To
Judy
All the
Best

Jim

jknisely@juno.com

CHANCE

An Existential Horse Opera

JAMES
KNISELY

mwynhad
SEATTLE

CHANCE
An Existential Horse Opera
Copyright © 2002 James Knisely.

mwynhad
1615 43 Avenue East #101
Seattle, Washington 98112
www.mwynhad.com

The characters and events portrayed in these
stories are fictitious. Any similarity to persons, living
or dead, is coincidental.

Cover design by Josh Knisely.
Interior book design by Stacy Wakefield
Printed by RPI Seattle, Washington

All translations from Virgil, *The Aeneid*, are by
the author or by Robert Fitzgerald.

ISBN 0-9657993-9-5
Library of Congress Catalog Card Number 2002105190

For Merilyn,
who brought this baby to life,

And especially for Lois,
whose patience showed me her love.

Horse opera *n.* **1.** A film or play about cowboys, cattle rustlers, etc, set in the American West. **2.** Any romance of the Old West.

Existential *adj.* **1.** Of or pertaining to existence. **2.** Pertaining to the philosophy of existentialism.

Existentialism *n.* The philosophy that recognizes the absurdity of the human condition as the very thing that makes it worthwhile.

PROLOGUE

In the film *Lonely Are the Brave*, the actor Kirk Douglas portrays a drifting cowhand who breaks into and then out of a small-town jail and makes a harrowing escape on horseback over the mountains only to be run over by a truck hauling a load of toilets. Not a true horse opera, perhaps, but certainly a horse-meets-truck opera; certainly a romance of the absurd.

Destry Rides Again is closer to the real thing. In that film the actress Marlene Dietrich gives her life to save the hero Jimmy Stewart. Yet in the novel of the same name she never even appears. I have always thought that gives the question of existence a curious turn.

Existence. In a time before the movie age they said the world was made of air, water, fire and dust. By the time of the talkies, though, we told ourselves we knew better. Roy Rogers knew about hydrogen. Gene Autry knew about carbon. Kirk Douglas even knew about plutonium.

But W.C. Fields, while not in quite the same mold, is said to have believed the world is made of just three things: oxygen, nitrogen, and baloney. I am not certain his view was supported by the science of his day, yet it stands now as a kind of paradigm: the paradigm of the existential horse opera.

PART ONE

He looked back to the ramparts, now glowing
In the flames of unhappy Dido's pyre; but what had
Caused so great a blaze he could not guess.

Virgil, *The Aeneid*
V, 3–5

I

A NASTY CHILL CREPT ALONG HIS BACK, DRIVING him toward a waking he did not want. His head pounded, and a half digested rodent stew churned madly in his stomach, trying to get out. He could tell that some of it already had.

As his eyes flickered open, a narrow glimmer appeared before him, floating between the horizon and the still dark reaches of the night. He sensed the quiet in the air and the smell of the waking prairie as the fringe of light began to grow and distant hills emerged from the dark.

He prayed as best he could through shivering and muttered oaths that numbness would overtake him, but of course it would not.

He lifted his head a little and watched the prairie start to spin around him. He was not impressed; spinning prairies were nothing new. Even so, he hated the spinning now as much as ever.

When he put his head back down, he discovered that he lay in a bed of dust. He lifted his head once more and snorted and spat and blinked his eyes, and ran a hand through his hair. The prairie whirled a little more, then settled slowly back to earth.

He managed to sit up. Everything throbbed. In spite of the cold, sweat poured from his skin and soaked his clothes, adding a perverse fuel to the shivers.

He looked around.

He was next to a rail fence. A corral. He guessed he was behind the livery, but wherever he was, he was alone.

He leaned into the fence and hoisted himself with difficulty to his feet. The prairie and the sky and the mulligan in his depths began their rolling and churning again as he hung from the toprail and shook with such violence he could barely hold himself up. He looked down at the pulverous earth beneath his feet and considered dropping back for a little rest, but he took a breath and thought things over and decided instead to find himself a drink.

He still wasn't sure where he was. He seemed to be at the edge of a town, though what town it was he couldn't recall. And he didn't especially care. All he really cared about was finding that drink.

He walked uncertainly hand-to-hand along the fence until he reached the other side of the corral, then peered down the street into the town. It was a spare, hardscrabble place with little pretense and no charm at all. The buildings were tall and lank for such a town. Some were separated by weed-choked little yards, and most opened without flourish onto the dust of the street. He didn't think he recognized it.

He let go of the fence and lurched toward the nearest building, across the front of the stable. When he reached the corner of the building, his legs began to wobble with a violence born of the shakes. He crashed against the building and into the street, then lay there sweating into the dirt until he passed out.

He dreamed the animals of the desert were playing a game at his expense. Several animals were there, various creatures of the deserts and prairies, lizards and gophers

2

and snakes, taking turns ramming him in the ribs with their heads, trying to see who could butt him the hardest without knocking himself cold. Dazed animals sprawled everywhere, strewn about the prairie near his body, against which they had inflicted cerebral contusions on themselves for sport.

But something else was there, too, something or someone, someone he could not see. He craned his neck and tried to see who it was. A man stood among the strewn creatures, a tall man whose face he could not make out, an old man, he thought, whose face he could not quite see.

The man approached without a word and stood over him in stark relief against the sky, then nudged him in the ribs with his boot, much as the creatures had done with their heads.

"Come on," the man said, poking him again. "Let's git up." He strained to see the man's face but could not.

The man took hold of him under his arms and raised him to his knees. Then, as everything began to spin and reel, the man lifted him to his feet. "Come on," the man said. "Git up."

He leaned against the building and opened his eyes. Before him stood a man not so tall and not so old, but powerfully made, with a great mustache and eyes as gray as his hair—and on his coat the silver badge of the law. He knew at once that meant no drinks today.

"I figured when I told you to move on you might not git far," said the law. "I don't expect you'll be going too far this morning, either."

The marshal wrapped an arm around his back, supporting him under the arms so he wouldn't reel away and crash through someone's storefront. They walked in this manner down the street to a squat adobe building between gangling structures in the center of town. The marshal opened the door and dropped him into a wooden armchair inside.

3

"Most likely you'll be going on the hospitality of the county for a few days," the marshal said. "I'll put the coffee on before I book you. I guess you could use a shot of that, eh?"

"Thanks," he said. The sound was closer to a croak than a word.

The marshal puttered about lighting a blaze in his firebox, then put the coffeepot on to boil.

He didn't move. He felt about as bad as a man could feel—and he wanted a drink about as bad as a man could want.

"Now, then," the marshal said, looking for some papers in his desk. He found them. "Name?" he said.

He didn't answer right away. His mouth moved a couple of times, but no words came out. His mouth and throat felt like dust. He needed a drink.

"Your name?" the marshal said.

His mouth moved again, but only a sticky sound came forth. He wasn't quite sure why. He took a breath, then tried once more. His voice rattled like a gust of wind in a screwbean tree, but this time he heard it form a word.

"Chance," he heard it say.

He stifled a laugh when he heard what he had said. He didn't know why that single word, of all the possibilities of the human tongue, was the one that escaped just then from his. He had no idea what his name was, and wasn't sure he cared.

"Howzzat?" the marshal said, and he realized the sound may have been closer to a croak than a name. He said the name again, carefully, and the marshal wrote.

"First name?" the marshal said.

"Ebenezer," he said. Now he nearly laughed out loud when he heard what he had said. He had no idea where that name had come from, either. A Bible name, he thought. Ebenezer. So for now that was his name, too. He didn't care.

4

"Where you from, Chance?" the marshal said.

He couldn't think of where he was from any more than what he was called. What he did know was that he needed a drink. He knew a drink would clear his mind; he also knew the marshal would not agree.

"Kansas," he said. He sat up with a start when he realized they might be in Kansas even then. He had no idea where he was.

"Waal, I don't seem to have no paper on you, Chance," the marshal said. "I know I'd remember that face. Man with your face and your liquor habit wouldn't stay at large for long. You wanted for anything anywhere?"

He wasn't sure what the marshal meant about his face. He ran a hand across it and thought about the question.

"I wouldn't guess I'm wanted anywhere for much at all," he said. He managed a twisted smile at his own joke.

"No," the marshal said dryly. He got up. "I ain't got much in the way of rooms, Chance, but I believe I can find you a bunk for now. I'll have Deputy haul you over to Tucker when you're able. Circuit judge meets there. I imagine they'll want a few days' labor for your keep."

The marshal showed him into a grim little room and locked him in. "There's blankets there and a bucket on the floor. I'll bring you coffee when it's done."

With the cell beginning to whirl around him, he found the blankets and managed to crawl under them. Once more, still cold and sweating, he passed out.

Three days elapsed before the shaking and the spinning and the onslaughts of the creatures wound slowly down. On the fourth day the deputy, a seedy dirt farmer named Rabie who gave the marshal a hand from time to time, took him the half-day ride to the town of Tucker, where they had a real jail and a kind of courtroom and public work for convicts.

5

The ride was a disagreeable trek through South Texas wasteland that could have passed for hell. He was still weak and giddy and subject to fits of the shivers, and as if that were not enough, he was obliged to ride with his wrists in irons.

He managed to reach the Tucker jail without pitching from his mount. He was glad to be safely locked in his cell, a kind of homecoming after all; he couldn't recall having been in that jail before, but he understood that home was wherever he parked his hide.

He still wanted a drink, especially after that ride, but he felt he might live without it for a while. For the time being, just resting seemed pretty good.

Still calling himself Chance, he was convicted of things he understood too well, and sentenced to work on a bridge just out of town. He was feeling a little better and didn't mind the work. The food in jail was edible, the tortillas and beans of South Texas, and the bunk was hard, the way he liked it. And his mind seemed to be growing clearer.

But it wasn't right. He couldn't remember who he was or where he came from or what he had been doing before his drunk.

And he couldn't remember his name. That worried him most. He realized he must have put away a lot of whiskey to reach that state, and might need some time to find his way back. He also knew that with so much drinking under his belt, he might do just as well not to go back.

He was alone in the Tucker jail almost a week. Then one night his sleep was disrupted by the arrival of another guest. Chance couldn't see the man, who was carried in and laid out in another cell, but he knew the man was there from his snoring.

The new man joined him at the bridge a couple of days later, a peculiar old-timer with a hawklike face and a lean and bony frame. He was not a drifter like Chance, just a

6

timeworn soakhead whose drifting days were done. Their keepers called him Toejam, a name he did not dispute.

Toejam was a good old man, and Chance found no meanness in him. Yet watching Toejam was like watching himself a few years down the line, he thought, and he didn't much like what he saw. Working with Toejam was making him uneasy. Working with Toejam was making him want a drink.

Though Chance did not get his drink, the men stopped in the morning heat for water.

"Where you from, Chanct?" the old man said. There was something odd about the question, as if he were somehow driven to ask it of everyone he met: "Where you from, Stranger?" But Toejam was an odd old man; maybe he too was trying to remember where he was from.

"Lot of places," Chance said. "Wherever there's cows." That much he knew.

Toejam squinted as he looked into Chance's face. "I been thinking I seen you before," he said. "Long time ago. Up north, mebbe Wyoming, Montan."

"Could be," Chance said. "I reckon I've worked here and there." He was suddenly curious about what the old man might remember.

Toejam wiped his forehead with a shirtsleeve. "You don't mind my saying, son, you got a mighty particular face. No offense, but shore it seems like one a body would recall, even after fifteen–twenty years of hard likker."

At this the old man broke into a fit of wheezing so violent it took Chance a moment to realize that this was Toejam's laughter.

"I know I've seen your face before," Toejam said when the wheezing had stopped, "but I'll be damned if I can remember the rest. I weren't such an old cuss then. I don't reckon you'd remember."

"Sorry," Chance said. "Maybe your face ain't as particular as some." Toejam flew into another attack of his frenzied wheezing as they went back to work.

The bridge was a log setup that straddled a creek not far from the town. It had been damaged by flooding, and a crew of four men had been assembled to reset the footings. The work was hard in the sun but felt good to Chance, who found he liked this sweating better than the other. It wasn't as kind to Toejam, but he bore the strain with the salt of a man who had worked hard in his life. Maybe in a way the sweating was good for him, too. When they returned to the jail at night, they turned in early and slept hard.

One night Chance heard a voice crying out in the distance, a strange and wind-borne voice calling his name from far away. "Chance," it called to him. "Chance."

The voice crept closer in the night as Chance rose from the abyss of sleep. "Chance," the voice cried; "Chance."

As he struggled free of sleep Chance recognized the voice of Toejam, wheezing from his cell.

"Chanct," the old man wheezed between the bars.

Chance got up and tried to press his face through the bars of his cell. He couldn't quite make Toejam out.

"Chanct," the old man said. "It come to me. I figgered 'er out. By Gawd, she come to me."

"What the hell are you talking about," Chance said, though he already knew.

"I remember now," Toejam said. "Been twenty year or more, but I knowed I remembered that face. Gawd dang, ain't that somethin', after all them years..."

He was interrupted by the night deputy, who had been sleeping out front.

"Stifle the chatter," the deputy bellowed from the office, "or y'all could get plumb hungry come breakfast."

"Where?" Chance whispered.

"Montan," Toejam wheezed. "Up in Montan. It finally

8

come to me. By Gawd, I knowed I'd seen that face before."
He was out of breath now and could hardly wheeze. Chance
listened as the old man shuffled back to his bunk.

Chance stood at the bars a while longer, pressing his
face into the spaces and trying to remember. But the past
was simply a fog in his brain, and the word Montana little more than a sound. He tried to think about Montana,
to picture it in his mind, to be there once more, but he
could not.

"Tomorrow, Jam," he whispered. "Tell me tomorrow." He
leaned against the bars a few minutes more, then went
back to bed.

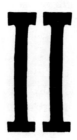

II

AN OLD EXERCISE IN THE LOGIC TEXTS ARGUES that a baloney sandwich is better than complete happiness. The argument is disproved, of course; yet there are times when even a baloney sandwich looks pretty good.

In the morning Toejam was not with the crew that went to the bridge. They told Chance the old man was being released. Chance spent the day brooding about this turn of events; he hadn't wanted to let Toejam get away before finding out what he knew.

Chance thought all day, working in the heat of the sun, trying to remember something of his past, anything, any spark or inkling that might remind him who he was. When he got back to the jail, the old man was gone as well. Chance cursed him and the perversity of luck, and thought about getting drunk when he got out.

When the bridge was done, Chance finished out his sentence in his cell. He found the boredom harder than working; he didn't even have his memories to help him through the days and hours. Yet he was not entirely without his thoughts. He did have one notion with which he whiled away his time: the shred of a possibility of a distant and hazy past.

So Montana loomed in his mind, if obscurely, as both a shimmering range a thousand miles away and a mystery based on the recollections of an old man. There had been something remarkable in the memory that had come to Toejam in the dark, something extraordinary. Chance had heard it in his voice. He had to find out what it was, before that washed away from Toejam's memory, too, perhaps for good.

They kept him for a week after the bridge job was done. Then one morning the deputy turned him out.

Chance was flat broke with no horse and no place to go. He needed a job. He believed he could get one easily enough—but first he had some unfinished business.

He found the town of Tucker a little livelier than the place where he had woken up drunk a month before. No one paid him much heed as he stepped into the street to look for the saloon.

He found it just up the street from the jail. He stopped in front for a moment before going in.

The place was empty. At the bar he looked at the rows of bottles. They had Kentucky whiskey there, another connection with the past: he knew he loved good Kentucky corn. He tried to think of a way he could come up with the price.

"Help you?" the bartender said.

"Looking for a feller, may hang out around here. Old waddie, goes by Toejam."

"Sure," the bartender said, wiping the bar with a yellowish towel. "You a friend of his?"

"Met in the *juzgado*," Chance said.

"Well, no harm, I reckon. Lives just out of town east of here. Real small place, kinda run down, if you know what I mean. Lives there with his son. Can't miss it. The Early place. Just out of town on the right."

Chance thanked the man and looked at his bottles

11

again, then turned away and walked out into the sunlight of the street.

Toejam's place lay out the main road in the opposite direction from the bridge. The country there was flat and nearly treeless, and dusty in the sun. Chance didn't like being on foot in such country.

About a mile from town he came upon a dusty shack among some scrubby oaks just off the road to his right. Some chickens wandered in the yard, and a small garden wilted off to the side. He was met in the yard by a thin yellow mongrel that flapped its tail more like a cow than a dog.

Chance shouted toward the house. The only response was the drowsy tail-waving of the dog. He stepped to the door and shouted again. This time he heard grunts and scrapings inside, and Toejam appeared in the door.

"Caught me napping," the old man said. "Figgered you'd be by. Step on in."

The cabin stunk, not with the odors of a wretched old man, but as if Toejam for some inscrutable reason kept the walls and furnishings of his home rubbed with garlics and leeks. It seemed his garden produced garlic in abundance, but little else. He kept the garlic in barrels under the house, but even so, the heat of the day had a vaporous effect.

Two bunks crowded the tiny room, along with a sticky-looking table and a rusty potbelly in the corner.

Toejam motioned for Chance to sit at the table. "Just get out?" he asked. Chance nodded. Toejam waved his arm toward the room. "My boy Ukiah's place," he said. "'Tain't much, but it keeps us. He's working over to the Lowman place these days. We don't get a lotta company out here."

"Well," Chance said, "seems to me we was interrupted last time we spoke." He sat down in a spindly chair at the table.

Toejam gasped and wheezed as he had before, his man-

12

ner of laughing. "So we was," he wheezed. "Seemed a matter of some weight to you."

"I ain't remembering much these days," Chance said. "Too long on the *buzo*, maybe."

Toejam ran his hand through his hair. "My own rememberance ain't as good as she uster be," he said, "but I knowed I'd seen you before, and it finally come to me that night. Course your face weren't quite so stove up in them days. I reckon it's seen a hoss-hoof or two since then, but it were the same face, I'd bet on it. Up in Montan, it were. I must have been about your age at the time, and you was just a young buck. You was still working your pappy's spread, before they tooken it. I was working for old man— what was his name? Larson, I think, some such name as that. Remember old man Larson?"

Chance gazed blankly toward the past and shook his head.

"Old man Larson," Toejam said and licked his lips. "Next spread over from yours. Stole your place from you, lock, stock and powder. Your pappy's ranch. Don't that bring it back?"

"Stole our ranch?" Chance sat there at the table in a stifling little shack belonging to men named Toejam and Ukiah somewhere in Texas, staring across the timeless spaces of that room and trying to cut through the fog that had consumed vital regions of his brain. "You'd think I might remember a thing like that, wouldn't you?" He stared out through the fog.

Toejam licked his lips again and waited for Chance to remember, but Chance only shook his head. "I can't," he croaked. "It just ain't there no more."

"Jesus Criminy," Toejam said. "Wal, lemme tell you leastwise what I can.

"I was working for this here old man Larson." He fished a once-red handkerchief from a pocket and dabbed it across his brow. "There were some unpleasantry between the Larsons and y'all, and also the bank, which had took the

13

side of the Larsons. I cain't recall exactly, but I remember thinking the banker and the Larsons stood to be a sight richer from the arrangement. Your pappy obliged them by dying in the midst of it all."

A dusty light filtered through the room from its only window. "I reckon your pap was the first rancher in them parts," the old man said. "Biggest ranch in the Montana Territory, as I recollect. Larson was a pard of his from the old days, so he staked him to an outfit of his own, but some said he trusted Larson too far and paid with his own ruin. I don't know about that, but shore he paid Azrael's price, and you wound up minus your pappy and your ranch and dang near everything else.

"I believe you lit out after that, swearing vengeance on them that done it, and I never seen or heard of you again—till now, of course—though it seems I heard one time that old man Larson had been bushwhacked. It did cross my mind to think that there bushwhackin' might have bore your hand in it, but I never rightly heard."

Chance sat at Toejam's table with his elbows sticking to it and his open hands on either side of his nose propping up his head. He stared past his hands, still trying to capture the past. His mouth began to move dryly, as it had the morning his name would not come, and again he tried to speak words that would not form.

He took a breath, then slowly let part of it out.

"What were we called?" he finally asked. "What was our name?"

"Your name," the old man said, looking out the window as if Chance's family name might be out there somewhere in his garlic patch. "Your name. Waal now, lemme think about that. Larson, I think. Larson. Something like that."

Chance came up off the table like a toad off a hot rock, nearly leaving patches of elbowcloth behind. "Larson!" he roared. "You crazy old fart, you said Larson was the other

14

one—the one *you* worked for!"

A foolish grin seized control of Toejam's face; Chance could see his features change color even in the murky light of the shack.

"I reckon that's what I said," he admitted.

"Come on, Toejam, what's the truth of it? Get it right, now, damn you—I gotta get this straight."

Toejam shifted uneasily in his chair. "I told you, Chanct, I disremember it some myself. But somebody in the deal was Larson, one of them names. I wisht I could remember it better for you."

"What *do* you remember, then? How much of this here memory of yours is good and how much is blue loco? Don't spin me no yarns, *Viejo*—I have to know what you remember."

Toejam looked past Chance out that pitiful window. "I'm remembering two things for shore," he said. "One is yourself. I told you before, I ain't never forgot your map. It were you all right, just took me a day or so to place you. The other thing is this: they stole your spread. I reckon I knowed it at the time, and I didn't like it. I ain't never liked to see a man beat of what he's sweated for, but it warn't none of my concern, and soon enough I moved on to other spreads and other men's problems. Not to mention my own."

With that he flew into one of his wheezy fits. They always began as a laugh and ended as a seizure that seemed to threaten the old man's life.

"Waal now," he wheezed when he had begun to catch his breath, "mebbe a little medicinal aid is in order." He wheezed a little more for effect. "Have a tetch?" He got up from the table and looked at Chance as if he held the key to celestial bliss and needed only an earthly blessing to swing it wide. Chance remembered the taste of good whiskey and thought of having a sip with Toejam.

"No," he said.

15

The word sounded as if it had dropped in from another planet. Chance was as surprised as Toejam, who cocked a thinning eyebrow in disbelief.

"No thanks," Chance said, looking intently again through the dim light toward the past.

"Ah, hell then," Toejam said, waving his wadded handkerchief in a gesture that seemed to mean several things at once.

He dabbed the handkerchief at his forehead once more, then stuffed it back into his pocket and dipped a cup of water from a bucket. He drank from the dipper then returned it to the bucket and sat back down at the table. "So what's your plan?" he said. "You can always get work, I reckon, eh?"

"Yes," Chance said, "I reckon. I may start drifting north a little. This story about your Larson clan has kinda struck my fancy. Something to look into, anyway. Up in Montana, you say?"

"Hell, Chanct, it were long ago by now. Yeah, Montan, I reckon, Wyoming, up in there. But hell, you won't find nobody to remember it no more. Not after all these years. Mebbe I don't remember it so well myself."

Chance peeled his shirtsleeves more carefully from the table this time and stood up. "I'll remember that," he said.

Chance decided he would do himself a favor by not staying with old Toejam and his son—and would probably be doing them a favor as well. He needed work. He got directions to the Lowman outfit and took off on foot, hoping to get there by dark. He faced a walk of several miles in the heat, but he felt good—and he felt himself being pulled by something he didn't yet understand.

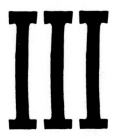

III

CHANCE WORKED ENOUGH TO GET HIMSELF A long-toothed dun and little silver in his jeans. Then, with a few biscuits and a couple pounds of beans, he headed north. He had no idea he was riding into an existential horse opera, or indeed that he was riding into any horse opera at all. Had he known, he might well have decided to take his chances where he was.

As he drifted, he worked more than he rode and found that he liked the work. He answered one question about himself for sure: he had done this work before.

He took an odd pleasure from discovering the kinds of things he had forgotten and those he remembered. Cowherding he remembered as well as if he had never been away. Geography he remembered too, even history. The only things he couldn't remember were the personal ones: where he was from, what he had done in his life beside punching cattle, who he was. That single part of his mind had drifted loose like a pigweed in a storm.

At night on the prairie Chance lay sometimes for hours beneath the endless Texas heavens thinking the thoughts that come to all men when they lie among the starry depths. But he was not like other men; all he really knew of himself was his love of lying under the stars and waking in the chill stillness of dawn and working cattle and loving women.

And the thing he loved most of all, and feared most: whiskey.

All the same, he had that one thing he thought perhaps no other mortal had beneath the stars—the misty legend of betrayal and revenge wheezed at him one afternoon by an old man in a reeky shanty somewhere far behind. So he worked a few weeks here and a month or two there and drifted north following the cattle and the stars.

As for women, he withheld himself, denied himself, as if he needed time to discover himself before he could offer himself to a woman—time and a certain distance from that terrible corral where his recognition of himself began.

But there is a time, the Bible says, for everything—so in time, in a dirty cowtown along the Colorado River, Chance sought the comfort he needed.

The woman—a girl, really—worked a cowpoke saloon called the Bull and Beast. Chance bought her a drink. She called herself Starla, and made a kind of small talk with him until she finished her whiskey and took him upstairs.

Starla was not only young but rather pretty for a woman of her trade. She had dark, shadowy eyes and a mouth so small Chance almost wondered how she ate. Other parts of her were not so small.

Her room was cramped and shabby. The wallpaper, a once-elegant print of ladies and parasols, was darkening into yellow and brown. The bed was not made, as Chance felt he liked beds to be; it simply lounged there half open, like a desert flower waiting for the dawn. Starla sat on the edge of the bed and took off her shoes while Chance stood dumbly in the middle of the floor.

"Well?" she said, looking up from the bed. Her eyes made something inside him want to melt.

"Yes," he said, not remembering the protocol. "How much?"

"Two bucks a dance, ten for the night. I know you got it, I already seen." Her hair was dark and fine, and Chance was pleased to think it also looked clean.

"Yes," he said again, and took off his shirt.

Starla stood up and slipped off her clothes, then started to get into the bed.

"Wait," Chance said. "Stand up." She looked at him with a trace of apprehension, then stood up by the bed.

He remembered what women looked like, but couldn't remember ever having looked at one. Excitement centers in his nervous system sprang to life as he had a look at this one.

She had as good a shape as he could imagine. Her waist was so tiny he thought he could circle it with his hands, but she wore as nice a pair of lungs as he believed he had ever seen. Chance could hardly wait to see them a little closer, and maybe touch them some, and so on.

He took his boots off so as not to step on her feet, then put his hands around her little waist and bent down to kiss her little mouth.

She turned her face to the side. "Huh-uh," she said. "No kissing. It ain't sanitary."

He shrugged but kept his hands on her waist. "All night," he said.

She turned her face back to his. "Is that right," she said, then kissed him in the most incredible way. He thought he would have remembered being kissed like that; it was a kiss that carried him far away. She slipped out of his hands and into the bed, and he shed his breeches and joined her before she had even settled.

When they were done, Chance held her for a while. She lay with her silky hair falling on his chest and his shoulders

19

and his face. She felt good to him, she made him feel alive—yet as he held her he realized that he was leaking tears into her hair.

He couldn't remember the last time he had been with a woman. He couldn't remember any woman he had ever been with. He couldn't remember whether there had ever been someone important or whether there was someone like that even now, wondering what had become of him under the Texas sky. He doubted that. Now here he was with this pretty young woman, prettier than the women he had seen in other towns like this, and she felt better to him than anything he could imagine.

As Starla became aware of his weeping, she began to rock him in her arms. And she began to whisper to him.

"Thank you," she whispered. She looked at him and wiped his tears with her fingers and brushed his hair from his face and rocked him in her arms. "Thank you," she whispered as they rocked. "Thank you. Thank you." And before Chance knew it, he was asleep.

Starla didn't have to be downstairs until noon, so in the morning they made some more loving. She was good at what she did, yet that morning she seemed somehow different. She brushed his hair from his face as she had before and looked into his eyes.

"You okay?" she said.

He remembered what he had done. "Sure," he said, and let her brush his face.

"I like you," she said. "You're nice. It feels good with you."

She asked him a few things about himself and didn't seem puzzled by his answers. She had probably heard answers like them before. But she did seem to like him, and she wanted to talk.

She told him she was from St. Louis. She had come to Texas with a young man who wanted to be a cowboy. He

20

had been hanged for stealing a horse, so there she had stayed.

She asked him if he wanted more loving, but he kissed her and ran his fingers through her hair and told her he wanted some breakfast. When he was dressed, he paid her the ten dollars and kissed her on the head.

She looked up at him. "You come back again," she said, "you hear?" Chance said he would, and was sure he would do just that.

Complete happiness. That seems like a lot to ask for, of course, and a baloney sandwich is probably a safer bet. Yet a *little* happiness seems like a fair request—and seems so often just within reach.

Ten dollars was a lot of money, so Chance didn't get back to see Starla as soon as he wanted. A two-dollar throw really wasn't what he had in mind, so he decided to save up the ten. He got a job with a small outfit not far from town, helping with some branding they had just started.

He wanted to see Starla again, and only Starla would do. There was something about her, and she stayed in his mind even as he worked.

The outfit he was working for paid at the end of the month, and in a couple of weeks he had another twenty. He found himself at the Bull and Beast on a Friday night, standing at the bar while he looked the women over and contemplated getting himself a drink. When the bartender came, Chance ordered coffee. Starla wasn't in sight.

"Buy me a drink, cowboy?" A woman took his arm and drew herself close, a red-haired hustler who might once have been good-looking, though she was still far from old.

"Thank you ma'm," Chance said, and bought her the drink. "Tell you the truth, I'm looking for someone."

The woman didn't seem to mind, and tendered the customary patter while she sipped her whiskey.

There were two kinds of saloons in the Texas cowcountry: those with whores and those without. Some were little more than shacks that served whiskey, but the Bull and Beast boasted crimson velvet on the walls and a mirror behind the bar and varnished woodwork everywhere. And women. Eight or ten of them. At the moment Chance was only interested in one.

Someone took his other arm while he was talking with the red-haired whore. "This cowboy taken?" she said. The redhead was about to object when she understood. She tossed her whiskey back and gave Chance a wink, then slid away to find another drink.

Starla pressed herself into Chance's arm. "Chance," she said. "Where you been all these weeks? I been watching for you."

"Saving my cartwheels," he said. He could feel her warmth flowing through him. "A drifter don't have much chance to get ahead."

"I reckon a girl don't either," she said. "I'm glad you come back."

He bought her a drink, and himself another coffee. When they were finished they went up to her room. She was as pretty as he remembered. He smiled at having something to remember. And he smiled when she put her hands behind him and took him by the small of his back, then closed her eyes and kissed him as she had before, and carried him away to places he knew he had never been.

They lay in bed afterward as they had before. Holding this woman made him happy. The ten dollars was hard to part with because he needed his wages to get him north to Montana, but being with Starla had brought him the first happiness he could remember. Ten dollars didn't seem too much to pay for a little happiness.

Starla lay on top of him and brushed his face with her fingers and looked into his eyes.

22

"You ain't cryin'," she said.

"I reckon not," he said.

"Why was you really cryin' before? Was it really just because of me?"

He told her he had cried because of her and because he had a passion for beauty and because her loving was the most beautiful thing he had ever known. It was not untrue, and made her smile. They talked into the night, more about her than him, of course, and she seemed to like him. They made love again, then went to sleep, and parted in the morning much as they had before. She kissed him with a passion of her own, and asked him to come back sooner. Her eyes told him she really did want to see him again.

He started making some of those two-dollar calls. At times they lingered a little, though not really to talk. Soon Starla said she wouldn't take his money any more, but he made her take it. "Customer is always right," he said.

Then one night Chance stayed with Starla again, and then they talked.

She was tired of the life; she had never liked it anyway. She had thought of going back to St. Louis, though to what she didn't know.

"But you know what?" she said. "I'm afraid here. Jesus, Chance, this ain't no place. You seen them girls down there."

She was sitting up in the bed, pretty as Chance had ever seen her, her shadowy eyes searching the little room. She turned toward him and searched his face.

"I can't go on here, Chance," she said. "I ain't regretting this, it's kept me alive. And it brought me you." She looked into his eyes as she had before. "But I can't go on doing this. I just can't do it no more." She touched his face and looked into his eyes, then leaned into his arms. They held each other for a long time without speaking.

He dreamed that night of a tall man, a troubled and

23

troubling old man. The man wanted something, expected something, and Chance did not know what it was.

The following day Chance was haunted by the eyes of the woman. Starla's face hovered in his mind much as it had at times before, but now her eyes seemed to follow him as he worked. He was growing attached to this young woman, and now she was asking him to take her away.

He knew they couldn't drift together, but they could hardly settle where they were. Maybe they could move up into the Panhandle somewhere and settle there. He liked that. She had touched something inside him, and he liked the idea of not having to share her with the other dirty and often vile men of the range.

But he began to grow restless, too. He understood that he could either settle with Starla somewhere or go to Montana alone, but he saw with growing conviction that he could not do both. A restlessness that felt like something old and familiar gnawed at him as he tried to avoid her eyes, and the happiness he thought he had found began to shrivel in the glare of his thinking.

He needed a drink. Montana could wait, perhaps, and maybe even the woman, but he needed a drink now. Yet the eyes watched, and he felt his sensibilities dividing themselves like warring factions between those that dwelt on the eyes of the woman and those that remembered the taste of whiskey.

It was no contest. He decided to go into town that night for a drink. A drink would clear his thoughts; a drink would drive the eyes from his mind. The moment he made that decision he felt better about everything.

After the meal that night Chance told the foreman he was shoving on. He collected his pay and saddled up the dun, but he did not go to town and did not get that drink. He rode north, and spent the night under that vast empti-

24

ness he loved, absent whiskey and absent woman. He thought about Starla: such a sad, pretty thing. He thought of those eyes once more, and a spark of regret flared along the fibers of his system. But he was going north again, and he knew he wouldn't be back.

IV

IN ABILENE CHANCE JOINED A DRIVE OF GRASS-fattened longhorns north into Kansas. Trail driving was very nearly a memory; he could almost remember how much he hated eating and breathing and wearing the dust of the herd.

At Dodge City he collected his pay but didn't stay to spend it. He followed the old Santa Fe Trail into Colorado, where he picked up a little work shoeing horses. But he didn't stay in Colorado either; he wanted to get on into Wyoming before winter.

He found himself in Casper by first snowfall. Casper, Wyoming proved a dreary place to winter. The cold and the snow were bitter, and the wind more bitter still. The buildings, weathered and tired, lined the streets like the flanks of dry gullies, down which the wind never ceased to blow.

Even the beautiful times of winter were ugly in that town. And Casper offered nothing for the passing of the days and the restless nights but work and drink and uninspired women. Chance managed to find work cooking and washing dishes in a hostelry known as the Brown House, and generally spent a cold but quiet winter without drink.

He inquired of everyone he met about the Larson ranch.

26

No one had heard of such a place. He grew morose in the long, dull nights and wondered why he had come.

The lodgers of the Brown House generated such entertainment as they might by the custom of swapping yarns. One evening Chance found three or four of them in the parlor doing just that.

The place had a new boarder named Homer Graf, a drifter like Chance, who said he had spent his life cowboying in Montana. Homer Graf was a tall man with an enormous mouth and a twinkle in his eye, who was cut from the same homespun as his clothes. He hadn't said much in the few days he had been at the Brown House, but with the attention of the place on spinning tales, he came to life.

His voice gave fair warning that he was a storyteller born—a voice full of color and mischief that seemed to resonate from chambers just below his ears.

Not to disappoint, he plied the others with stories of the early days of ranching in Montana, though he couldn't have been more than a child at the time. He rehearsed wild histories and spun amazing yarns of the wars with the Blackfeet and the Sioux, and of the heroes and the madmen who had built the ranches of the North.

Chance took in every word, but Homer gave no hint of the single history Chance craved. As the evening grew late he inquired at last if Homer knew of the Larson ranch.

"Well, now," Homer said, "I believe I do. What makes you ask?"

Thunder rumbled through Chance's brain. In less time than it took him to blink, he was on the edge of his seat. He recounted Toejam's story of a ranch which had been stolen from those who had built it up, and of a missing heir who it was said might one day return to take up his claim, and asked Homer if the Larson ranch he knew was such a place.

"Why," Homer said, leaning back in his seat and stretch-

27

ing out with his hands behind his head, "I expect everyone in Montana knows the story of that particular ranch. Paradise Ranch, it was called in the old days, which controlled so much grass and water between the mountains and the horizon that the man who first ranched it believed he had found heaven on earth. But heaven it wasn't, I reckon, if heaven is taken to be a happy place."

Homer Graf continued to lean back in his overstuffed chair, looking mostly to the highbeamed ceiling of the Brown House parlor for whatever help his memory needed.

"This here rancher, whose name I can't recall, was a Major in the Texas Rangers or one of them bunches who had stole him a herd after leaving the outfit and run it into Montana when the range was still open and the graze was free and easy. Had him a hell of a time with the Blackfeet, but survived by sheer stubbornness and come to control pretty near all the grass and water in that there part of the world.

"But it was a fool's paradise," he said. He sat up and looked around at the group. "As you boys know, the laws pertaining to ownership and grazing rights are a little complicated, and are sometimes complicated a little further according to who owns the bankers and the politicians. This here fella had given the various deeds and grants by which he controlled his ranch to his lawyer for safekeeping, but a wealthy fella named Larson made the lawyer a better offer, and wouldn't you know, them deeds just seemed to migrate into the keeping of that same Larson."

Homer slipped back in his chair once more and spread his legs and folded his gigantic hands behind his head.

"The Major knew he had been bamboozled, but he couldn't fight the thing on his own. He had friends and connections in Texas, but he figured it would take more than a telegraph to bring help to Montana. He had a grown son, so he sent the son to Texas, but I reckon the son was

28

never seen in them parts again. Story was that the son took to whoring and gambling in Texas and forgot to come back with the help, but there was some said he was detained by those who didn't want the help in the first place.

"In the midst of it all, the Major mysteriously quit breathing. I never did hear the exact manner in which he quit, but I gather it was—what's the best way to put this— 'unexpected.' After a period of mourning, about fifteen minutes, I'd say, this fella Larson couldn't find anybody else to stand between him and the Paradise Ranch, so he was obliged to take it over, and maybe a little more, and Paradise was gone with the dust."

He sat up and stretched. "Just about bedtime," he said. He looked at Chance. "So there you are. After statehood, another outfit come into the region and began exercising influences of its own. I don't guess the competition was to Larson's liking, so there's been bad blood between 'em ever since. Paradise Ranch. Gone with the mist."

Never believe anything you hear, we are told, and only half of what you see. If Ebenezer Chance had been privy to the wisdom of that proverb, he may have improved his prospect of finding a little happiness. But even a fool can't close his eyes, so he would still have been left with one of the fundamental dilemmas of existential man: the question of which half to believe.

In any event, there it was, and even though Chance could hardly believe his ears, he believed. A great ranch had been stolen. A man had been betrayed, and maybe murdered. And maybe his son was still out there somewhere in the world, maybe only recently off the bottle and wondering where he was from.

When the thaw came, Chance started north toward the Powder River. He hadn't saved much money washing

29

dishes, and what he had saved had gone into supplies. The dun had been a good horse, but he was tired, and the winter hadn't helped. Chance traded him at the livery for an appaloosa colt with fire in his eye, but the trade cost him everything he had, and he knew he would have to find work again before he reached Montana.

He hired on with an outfit along the Bighorn Mountains just in time for the spring roundup. The appaloosa proved as good a cutting horse as Chance had hoped, and the foreman liked the way Chance handled a rope.

Starla's face still hovered in his thoughts from time to time, but not much now; he was too busy during the day and too tired at night to think about much at all.

He hadn't met the owner of the outfit, a woman known simply as the Widder, but one day she came out to roundup camp with the supply wagon.

She couldn't have been more than thirty-five, and she cut a figure that was good for the eyes. She had long chestnut hair which she wore in a braid, perhaps to accommodate her Stetson hat. She was a bit strong in the nose, he thought, but appeared to have a good shape. Chance was pleased to see that he worked for such a widder.

He didn't know much yet about the kind of boss she was. The outfit was run on the range by a man about ten years Chance's senior with the unlikely name of Several Williams. Chance found something familiar about the man, as if he might have known him before, but Williams didn't seem to know Chance at all.

The Widder spent the night with the wagon and the next morning with the roundup boss looking over the gather. She left with the wagon shortly after the noon meal.

The following day the men broke camp and moved north along the foot of the mountains. The country was hilly with grass and sagebrush, and pine trees here and there. The men finished the roundup and the branding, then drove the gather south along the mountains to the Widder's place.

They separated part of the herd for a trail drive. Chance agreed to stay on to move the rest of the herd into the mountains for the summer; he needed the money and wanted no part of the trail drive, especially as its destination was the railhead in Casper.

Before they could move the herd into the mountains they had to gather strays that had already wandered up the valleys. Chance liked cowherding in the hills and mountains of the north and was sure he had done it before. His head seemed to clear a little more as he worked, something he had not found washing dishes in Casper. He began to gain confidence in himself, both as a rider and as a man, a grownup among the dirtynecked youngsters that made up the bunkhouse of the EA ranch. The craving for drink came less and less often, even when the other hands went off to the cantinas down Crazywoman way.

But even as he grew stronger, he grew restless once more in the search for his memory. And as his mind struggled to grow clear, the image of a glistening empire to the north grew clearer still, the dream of a paradise of blue horizons, lost and waiting to be found. It came like a whisper in the night as he lay in the bunkhouse listening to the snores and farts of dirtynecked youngsters and trying to remember.

V

STARLA'S FACE STILL HOVERED IN HIS THOUGHTS from time to time, but not much now. And what, you might ask, ever became of the poor, sad waif he left so casually behind? Or has she simply vanished like the Lost River from the desert of the existential horse opera?

The first rule of the existential horse opera is that anything goes. Characters appear and vanish at the whim of an unpredictable narrator. Anything is possible. Yet within the artifice of the narrative a character is no more a disappearing river than he or she is a slab of baloney sausage; within the fictional world a character is as much a human person as you or I.

So the second rule of the existential horse opera is this: no matter what the narrator may do, we do not write each other off. If the narrator is willing, we may see Starla again . . . or not, as the narrator wills. But we, ignorant mooncalves though we be, we do not shrug each other off.

The EA Ranch lay against the foot of the Bighorn Mountains at the narrow mouth of a valley, the perfect spot for a ranch.

One Saturday as the outfit settled into its summer routine,

Several passed the word that anyone staying on the place for the evening was invited to the ranchhouse for supper.

The Widder's house stood on a knoll overlooking the stream at the mouth of the valley. The knoll was formed by the leveling of a broad ridge that descended from the mountainside where the valley opened onto the plain. Behind the house a stand of jack pines ran up onto the arm. The sheds and barns of the EA spread out across the mouth of the canyon below the house.

The house was a little different from the other ranch houses of Chance's memory. The building itself was made of hewn logs, squared off like heavy beams, common enough for ranch houses in those parts, especially on older places, a two-story structure with a roof of cedar shakes. Both stories had large windows all around, checkered with little glass panes.

The house was solid and built to last, and would have been handsome but for the portico of alabaster columns that appeared to have been stuck on the front of this log dwelling as a kind of afterthought. The columns radiated a grandiosity somewhere between the majestic and the absurd, and the building stood on its hill a magnificent oddity. The hands called it simply "the palace."

The younger men all had plans to go to town that night, but Chance didn't know how often he would be invited to supper with the boss, so he decided to stay. Several stopped at the bunkhouse that evening and walked with Chance up to the palace.

The Widder lived alone in the house with a Mandan maid named Bernadetta. Bernadetta let them in.

The parlor occupied the front of the house. The floor appeared to be hewn of the same timbers as the walls, and was covered with rich and fabulous rugs. Across from the door stood a fireplace of mountain granite.

The Widder came into the parlor wearing an apron.

33

She thanked the men for coming, then showed them back out to her veranda and offered them drinks. Chance was surprised at how easy it was becoming to say no.

The house held a commanding view of the operation just below and, to the south and east, the hills of the Powder River. The Widder owned very little land outright, but she did own the mouth of the valley, and so controlled the valley itself. The grassy hills to the east were open range, a thousand square miles of free grass.

While Chance was looking it over, the Widder came back to the veranda, this time without her apron, and showed them in to supper. "Dinner," she called it, in the manner of the gentry.

The dining room was at the rear of the house, behind the great fireplace, a low-ceilinged hall of logbeam grandeur. The three of them sat down at a table that could have seated twelve.

The Widder looked good, Chance thought. He had never seen her quite like this. She wore a white dress with lace at the collar and the cuffs and no bustle in the skirt. Her hair was piled up behind her head and looked nice without her Stetson. Her eyes were about the color of her hair, maybe a little darker. She wasn't actually what Chance would have called beautiful, yet she looked good—and there was something in her face he liked.

As soon as they had taken their places, the Widder offered them wine. Chance waved it off.

"You're of the Methodist persuasion, Mr. Chance?" she asked.

"No ma'm," he said. "Not as far as I know."

"Well, except for our Methodists, and a few Mormons we've had, I've never known ranch hands to be abstainers. I hope you don't mind my asking."

"Me and liquor was once partners," he said, "but we had

a falling out. Now we've went our separate ways, and I reckon we're both the better for it."

This brought a guffaw from Several, who seemed never to have heard of such a thing, but the Widder only smiled.

The Widder had fixed the meal, a steaming platter of porkchops with tureens of escalloped potatoes and seasoned green beans and baby onions in cream. She seemed pleased when the men attacked the food with polite but honest vigor.

During the meal she asked Chance more about himself, but there wasn't, of course, much more to tell, and he didn't want to go into what there was. He had already discovered his knack for turning anything into a gag, but now he retreated into the equivalent cowboy trait of reserve, a quality often evoked by women. From time to time the Widder put her hand to her chin and seemed amused.

"Several tells me you dab a good rope," she said.

"I expect I've been roping long enough to catch a critter or two when the need arises," he said.

"Our Mr. Williams here is something of a legend in these parts for his talent with the rope."

"Once upon a time, maybe," Several said.

"Waal, that there's a lotta man," Chance said. "I mostly confine myself to doing a cowpoke's work for a cowpoke's wages, and leave the manly stuff to the boys."

Everyone laughed.

The Widder went to the kitchen and came back with a silver urn. She poured coffee for her guests and herself, then set the urn on the table. She stopped beside her chair and paused with a hand on its back.

"Several and I have been talking about you," she said. "We like the way you work. We can use a top hand around here, at least through the fall. I don't know your plans, but if you'll stay I'll pay you top wages."

"Just through fall," he said, "or what?"

35

"Would you consider staying on?"

"Well thank you. I like your place right fine, but I was heading north and I expect I'll want to push on before long."

"Let me make you a proposition," she said. A strand of hair had slipped free of the chignon in which she wore it and hung down the left side of her face. She whisked it away. "If you'll stay through fall round up, I'll make you my top hand. I'd appreciate the help. What do you say?"

Chance looked at this pretty woman and thought about her pretty ranch. And about top wages.

He cleared his throat. "I have some business in Montana," he said, "but maybe it'll keep. I'll stay through roundup, but I'll want to be in Montana before she snows."

The Widder offered her hand. "Mr. Chance," she said, "we have a deal."

They all sat down and the Widder served the coffee.

"One thing Several hasn't told me," she said, "is your given name."

"If it's all the same," Chance said, "it's a name I never use myself."

"Well," she said, "I generally try not to call a man by anything he wouldn't call himself." She asked to be called Elizabeth, and thanked him for staying on.

The men left before dark. Chance whistled a tune as they walked down the hill. Dinner with the Widder had given him things he had not expected: a chance to know the boss a little; a better job with more money; and a taste of feminine charm for the first time in months. He thought about feminine charm, and whistled his jaunty tune.

There is a time to refrain from embracing, the Bible tells us, and a time to embrace. The next time the younger men went to town, Chance went along. His mind had filled itself with thoughts of embracing.

36

There were three sporting halls in town. One was preferred by the EA hands for reasons they didn't explain. It wasn't much of a hall: a clapboard shed with badly lit cribs. But the fare was good enough, and cheap.

Chance engaged an exotic woman calling herself Esmeralda. She had a dark and angular face with hair on her lip and a hint of Gypsy wildness in her eye. She didn't express an abundance of charm, but her embrace was a work of art. Chance believed her embrace left him a better person, though Esmeralda was not noticeably improved.

As he left Esmeralda that night he silently thanked the Widder. It was she, after all, who had put embracing into his mind. He smiled at the thought as he stepped out into the night, and thanked the Widder very much.

VI

SUMMER DUTIES ROTATED THROUGH THE BUNK-house. Three or four hands drifted the range to the south along the foot of the mountains, where the EA brand grazed with others. Some worked the valley, hauling cattle from the creek and keeping an eye out for beasts of prey, and some rode the country eastward to the Powder. Two or three remained at the ranch to tend the horses and keep the outfit running.

Chance liked the rotation. Riding line to the east, keeping the herd out of the bogs along the river, was often solitary work. Most of the younger hands disliked working alone, so Chance did it himself as often as he could.

The EA had two line shacks which were sometimes used by other outfits as well. Chance didn't often run into other cowhands in the camps, but when he did he swapped gossip and traded yarns and asked about Montana.

One evening in July he came in from a week of working the southern range with a hand named Tinker. They had used up their food and were hungry. The only other men on the place were Several and an older hand called Rathead, who did the cooking. Rathead warmed a pot of beans he kept for such occasions, and served the beans to the men with cold cornbread that was growing stale. But at least the coffee was fresh.

While they were still eating, two hands from the high country came in. Rathead cursed for having to warm more beans, but seemed pleased for the chance to get rid of the last of the cornbread.

The new men had found a couple of slaughtered calves. A cat had come down from the ridges and found the hunting easy. They had tracked it back upcountry, but lost it above the head of the valley.

Several decided to take Chance and the two men back into the mountains to hunt the cat, and went up to the palace to tell the Widder he would be gone.

In the morning they packed for a three or four day hunt and started up the valley. The trail followed the creek for several miles through open forest. Cattle roamed everywhere, lurking among the trees and wandering among the parks, browsing and chewing and doing the idle things cows do.

At the far end of an open flat the vegetation changed from the pines and grass of the foothills to the firs and underbrush of the mountains. The hillsides were still mostly pine and thin grass, but the river bottom was greener than bovine El Dorado.

At that point the trail split. The main branch stayed north of the creek. The other forded the stream and took off through the woods toward a pass a little way to the south.

Several wanted to follow the main valley with Chance into the high meadows. The other two men, an experienced hand named Willaree and an eighteen-year-old called Suffering Pete, had found the kills and the cat spoor up the other branch. Everyone agreed the cat was following the backbone of the range, raiding the valleys over the passes, and were afraid it might decide to stay where the hunting was best.

The four men camped at the fork, where they built their

fire in a clearing just above the stream. It was different from a prairie cowcamp; instead of the open spaces and the sweep of the sky, the place was closed in on every side by mountains and towering woods. Chance liked the roar of the stream tumbling by, and felt he had camped by streams like this before.

After they had turned in, Chance lay on his back listening to the creek and watching the stars beyond the tops of the trees. In the night the trees were half a mile tall, and the stars only a little beyond. Chance fell asleep just lying on his back and watching those trees and stars.

They ate a breakfast of bacon and biscuits at dawn, then split up and hit the trail. Chance and Several climbed all morning; the cattle thinned out, but still wandered hither and yon.

Just after noon the men emerged from forest into a meadow that swept the width of the valley and rose to a pass a thousand feet above. A handful of cattle were in evidence, but not as many as Chance had expected. Several believed the cat had frightened the rest back into the woods.

They roped a calf and tied it out in the meadow below the pass. They sat up at night to watch for the cat, and slept during the day, but if the cat was around, it did not take the bait.

After three nights in the open they gave up. They figured they had spooked the cat enough so it wouldn't come back down off the ridge as long as their scent remained. "More than one way to skin a cat," Several said.

The men slept through the morning, then packed their gear and started down. When they reached the fork they found that Willaree and Suffering Pete had already gone back.

"Shore am getting hungry," Chance said.

"Cookfire ain't crowded," Several said.

"Fine spot, this," Chance said. "Might as well spend the night, wouldn't you say?"

The older man glanced at the sky. "Only five, six o'clock," he said. "I've got work to do, even if you ain't."

"Aw, don't be such a grump. It's three hours back to the ranch. Besides, I've got something to discuss."

"Izzat right?" Several said. He pulled at his nose.

"Of course it's right, or I wouldn't of said so."

Several grumbled something about getting back before breakfast, but Chance could tell he had his attention.

They ate the last of their food, then spread themselves out on the earth.

"Well, *hombre*, what's on your mind?" Several said.

"What do you know about me?" Chance said.

"You're a ugly sonofabitch, if you don't mind my saying, but you know cows, and you seem honest enough. Not much more than I know about anybody else. Why? Is there more?"

"Well, you see, that's the question. I reckon I don't know no more about myself than you do."

"Haw," Several said, rising onto one elbow. "All I know is, you ain't the missing prince. What are you getting at?"

"Just this," Chance said. "I woke up drunk one morning a little over a year ago and my whole memory of myself was gone. I don't know whether I drank it away or what, but my memory was gone, and it ain't never come back in all that time. What do you make of that?"

"Gawd damn, you're pulling my leg, ain't you?"

"No, I'm afraid I ain't. That's why I don't drink no more. I can remember most everything about cowpunching and the like, but doggone if I can recall a single thing about myself before that morning in Texas." Chance grinned at the aging cowboy staring into his face. "I don't reckon I remember that too good, either," he said. "Last day I ever took a drink."

41

"Well, I'll be damned," Several said. "I never did take you for no Texan. Your talk has a little Texas, sure, but you wasn't Texas bred, I'd wager on that."

"May be. I couldn't tell you. But I met this old feller down in the Nueces country who said he remembered me from somewhere. Said he thought it was up thisaway, maybe Montana, long time ago. He seemed a little fuzzy about things himself, but he thought he remembered that I had been cheated out of my pappy's ranch and run out of the country. That's about all he could remember. Larson outfit, he thought, but he couldn't remember whether Larson was us or the one that got our place.

"Then this drifter in Casper tells me he knows of a Larson spread in Montana, and tells me the same story all over. And he says there's some sort of turmoil going on there yet, and Larson smack in the middle of it. Now don't that seem like some coincidence? I don't quite know what to make of it, but ever since I heard this, I've been dogged by the idea that my . . . I don't know . . . my destiny, I suppose, is tied up in it—that somehow everything that's mine is waiting for me there to come and take it back. I don't know, that sound loco to you?"

Several scratched the stubble on his chin. "I'll give you this: your face is plain rememberable. Anybody says he remembers your mug, I'd have to bet he ain't making it up. All the same, some of these old whiskeydicks will tell you the damndest lies and swear they're the Lord's own truth. I hope you don't mind my sayin', but a face like yours is all one of these old gaffers would need to concoct a real ballbuster."

"That occurred to me, sure, but they both told me the same story. Now don't that seem strange? What if it's true?"

"And what if it ain't?" Several's leathery face seemed to float in the dark, propped up as it was on one hand. Chance peered through the depth of the darkness and tried to study the face while he thought about the words.

"I don't know," Chance said, staring past Several's face now and into the forest of the night. "I figured I would just drift north until I reached Montana and find out for myself. But here I am hunting wildcats in the Bighorn Mountains, and I keep thinking maybe it's time to move on."

"Mebbe it is, then."

"What about this Larson place or the Paradise outfit or any of that? Ever hear of it? Or anything about bad blood in Montana?"

Several frowned and pursed his lips. "I'll tell you the truth, Chance, I ain't heard none of it. That don't mean it ain't so, I don't really know Montana. But I've been in this here country for fifteen years and I ain't ever heard of them outfits. We had a spate of feuding here a few years back, but even that's a thing of the past. Wasn't no Larson or none of that."

Chance lay on his back and listened to the rushing of the creek. He wanted to believe that Several knew less about this Montana business than he did, but he knew that sometimes less was more.

"Well, here's the problem," he said at last. "I like it here. If things was different, I expect I could stay in a place like this and be plumb content. But this thing won't leave me be. What happened there in Montan? Am I the one? Why can't I remember? And what if that Montana spread is really mine? What kind of man would just let his pa's ranch go?"

"Chance, I would never advise a man to turn his back on his kin. Or his birthright." He lay back and folded his hands behind his head. "But that was a long time ago, see? I don't guess I'd mess with it now. Unless you got nothing to lose, I wouldn't fool with the past—especially if you don't know what's back there."

"Sure," Chance said, "I say that to myself, but it won't leave me be. It's like there's something out there calling me

43

to take back what's mine—and maybe redeem myself, as well. A matter of honor, maybe."

"Honor," Several said. "I seen a killing over honor once. Hell of a lot it proved, either, except that some dumb bastard was a little slower in the elbow than another. And the other one was hung, and all the honor they had between 'em wasn't worth the sweat it took to bury 'em."

"This ain't the same," Chance said.

"How long ago was this supposed to be? Fifteen, twenty years? Look, everything has its time. A feud may last for twenty years, but I ain't so sure about no mystery. If your hand played out on you then, it's gonna be played out now. Maybe you left Montana for a reason and ought to leave well enough alone—and maybe you've never been there before. Either way, there can't be no more to it now than smoke."

Chance looked across at him and rubbed the side of his face. "Don't sound like you share my curiosity," he said.

Several rose up on an elbow once more. "Ah, hell, Chance, that ain't it. Sure it's a curiosity. If this was my curiosity, I reckon I'd be bothered too. I gotta give you that. But this here is what I'm getting at: you only got a few years before you're my age, a little old to start making your plans. Then if you ain't got your ranch or your name or whatever, what will you have? Likely you'll go on down that whiskey river like your pardner down there on the Pecos, telling strangers how you recognize 'em and how they was once heir to some great ranch in some godforsaken place, wherever they ain't at the time."

A little night breeze stirred the pines overhead. Chance could see their dark forms swaying gently against the dark and the stars of the sky.

"Listen to me," Several said. "Take it from an old hand who remembers the ranges he's rid: Either light outta here in the morning for Montana and find the truth—whatever

44

it is—and get it settled, or make up your mind to start over right here where you're at and let the past bury the past."

Chance lay there listening. He hadn't really considered staying, but he began to realize what he would be giving up if he left.

He folded his hands behind his head. The question seemed to be whether the future lay with the past or with the present. But he was too tired to come up with much of an answer. He decided that after some sleep he might come up at least with a better question.

Maybe it was actually the future that determined the past. His face teased itself into something like a frown and he snorted quietly. The future. He rolled over and before long he drifted off, carried away by the sound of the creek.

VII

A WISE MAN ONCE WROTE THAT EVENTS IN THE past may roughly be divided into those which probably never happened and those which do not matter. You would have had your hands full trying to sell that thought to Chance; yet perhaps there is a sense in which the past is a creation of the future.

Chance pondered the things Several had said. He realized that setting himself up on the EA would give him a place to come back to if the Montana business came to a dead end after all, so he decided to stay through fall round-up as he had agreed and then move on. But he thought and thought about everything Several had said.

Several had dinner with the boss twice a week, and from time to time the boss invited Chance to join them. They usually discussed business, which gave him a chance to learn something about the operation.

Chance didn't understand what kept this woman on the ranch. She was from the East. Her husband, also an easterner, had died on a trip east a couple of years earlier. She could have sold the place or hired someone to run it for her, but she had stayed. She seemed to like ranching and had learned the business well. Still, Chance could see that she was lonely in her palace, and that she counted on their visits.

One evening late in August he went up to have dinner with Elizabeth alone. Several had gone down to Casper, leaving Chance in charge of the bunkhouse.

Elizabeth wasn't going to sell any cattle after fall round-up. She hadn't gotten a good price in the spring but believed prices would rise the following year, especially if enough ranchers kept their beef off the market. Others agreed.

Over coffee the conversation took a new drift.

"Tell me about yourself," Elizabeth said.

"I'm a cowpoke," he said. "Ain't much more to tell." He avoided her eyes by looking at his coffee.

"That's what you said before. But there's *something*. You're certainly not from Texas—isn't that right?"

"Waal," he said, "I reckon that's where I was before I left."

She waited for him to tell her where he had been before that. "Come on," she said. "You're not getting off that easy."

Elizabeth hadn't asked him about his past since that first time he had met with her and Several. He had thought about what to say when she finally asked him again, but he hadn't thought of a thing. And nothing came to him now.

"I just ain't used to talking about myself," he said.

"I don't mean to pry," she said after a pause, "but tell me one thing, anyway. Are you wanted?"

He couldn't restrain a little burst of laughter. "No," he said. "Not as far as I know."

"Chance, you've done a good job here. I like the way you work with the men, and I'm hoping you'll stay. But I like to think I can trust the men that help me run this place, and that they trust me. We see a lot of men with secret pasts—you know how cowhands are. And I believe in giving a man a second . . . "

47

She stopped herself and laughed out loud. "Well," she said, still laughing, "you know what I mean. And in return, I expect some trust—and the truth."

"I'm not wanted, and that's the truth. I'll allow I had a vagrancy or a drunk now and then in my more extravagant days, but that's about it."

"Your extravagant days," she said a little wryly. "I'll bet you did. I just need to know that I can trust you these days. I think you're a good man, and Several agrees."

"I appreciate that, but tell me this: do you really believe in giving a man a second chance?"

"Yes, why?"

"Seems a little risky, is all. Some men ain't worth a first chance, and not too many deserve a second."

"Chance, I've been through difficulties of my own. There's an old saying: 'Not ignorant of misfortune, I have learned to help the less fortunate.'"

In the splitting of an instant Chance's mind was somewhere else, far across time and space, far from ranching in the American West.

"*Non ignara . . .* " he said, struggling to remember. "*Non ignara mali miseris . . .* something," he said.

Elizabeth looked as though she had seen great Caesar's ghost. Chance's own surprise was surpassed only by the look on her face. She touched her mouth for a moment.

"Where on earth did that come from?" she whispered.

He couldn't keep himself from smiling now. "Virgil, I reckon."

She stared. "But how . . . "

"I guess I didn't tell you—Virgil is my middle name."

"You are wanted, aren't you?" Her face was a comedy of confusion, and she fiddled with her hair. "Forgive me," she said, "but who *are* you? You don't have to tell me everything, just tell me who you are. How on earth do you know Virgil? And in Latin?"

48

Needless to say, Chance was wondering the same thing, but he was hardly ready to explain. In the months since he had lost his memory, he had shared his secret with only Several and an old man far away who by now had probably wheezed himself out of existence. It was not something he was ready to make known, and sure as hell not to a woman, least of all the Widder.

"I reckon I done a little bookreading when I was young," he said. "I expect they tried to shove some learning into me before they give up. But that was long ago—it don't amount to much no more."

She watched him with enough intensity to wither stinkweed and waited for more, but Chance could do no more than stare at the palm of his hand.

"Mr. Chance, you're holding out on me, and I'd appreciate the truth. Will you tell me the truth? Who are you?"

He didn't know what to say. He didn't think he had learned Virgil on the moonlit plains, though it couldn't have surprised him much more to learn that he had.

"Waal," he drawled, "honest to God, ma'm, there ain't much to know. I'm just a cowhand with a little booklearnin' who'd ruther drift around and hunt cows than spend his days a-readin'. Ain't that uncommon, really."

She screwed up her face at the obvious half-truth, but he only grinned. "Honest," he said.

"All right," she said. She was not satisfied, but she seemed ready to let it go for now. Chance knew she would come back to it again.

"And how about you?" he said. "How's a buckaroo boss come to know Virgil any better than anyone else?"

"Nice try, Chance, but I intend to know about you, one way or another."

"I reckon you know everything already," he said.

"That's precious little, Mr. Chance, but even though turnabout is fair play, I'll answer your question. One of us, at least, should be forthright, don't you agree?"

"Yes ma'm," he said.

"I was raised in Pennsylvania. My father was a mining tycoon. He wanted a son but never got one. My parents sent me away to school when I was young, Pamela Forsythe's Finishing School, but I'm not sure my father looked into it terribly well, because Miss Forsythe proved to be rather progressive, something my father certainly was not. We read the great modern thinkers such as Mr. Emerson and Mr. Darwin and Mr. Wilde."

His face must have reflected his ignorance, because she laughed abruptly. "I'm sorry," she laughed. "I didn't mean to presume. Never mind about Mr. Wilde."

She laughed again, and there was something in her laughter that he liked.

"I don't guess you really expected an oldfashioned cowhand to know your Mr. Wilde," he said.

"I don't guess so," she said, still laughing. "A very modern man, my Mr. Wilde. But never mind him. My favorite was Mr. Whitman:

> *A child said,* What is the grass? *fetching it to me with full hands."*

She stopped. "What is it?" she said. "Have I said something . . . ?"

"No," he said. "I expect I've read your Mr. Whitman somewhere along the line."

"I don't suppose I should be surprised that a cowboy who knows Virgil would be familiar with Whitman," she said. "At least he wrote in English." That made her smile. "So whom else do you know?"

"Don't rightly recall," he said, "I'm a mite rusty. Been a parcel of time—a cowpoke don't generally have a library along on the range."

50

"Well, there's a library on this range. I'd be happy to let you read, if you'd like. Maybe you'll enjoy reacquainting yourself with Mr. Whitman. I can get you my Whitman right now. Do you mind?"

This was a long way from anything he had expected at dinner with the boss, but he thought he should at least accept the offer. "That would be nice," he said.

She left the room and returned a couple minutes later with a large leather-bound book in her hands. She held it out like a loaf of warm bread.

"Chance, I have to tell you, this is quite a novelty, having a literate hand on the place—even one who shrouds himself in obscurity. And I expect I will have the truth about that. But for now I'm pleased to have you read my books. I hope you'll feel free."

It was as much a novelty to him as to her. He had discovered a link to his past, and Elizabeth had brought it up. She had put him in touch with a part of himself he had been unable to reach on his own; yet he couldn't judge how far to trust her.

"I hope you don't mind my asking," Elizabeth said, "but what will the other men say about your bringing poetry books from the Widder into the bunkhouse?"

Chance grinned. "Oh, I can handle the boys," he said.

Chance left the palace early and returned with Whitman to the bunkhouse. Some of the hands were reading the magazines and novels that circulated from ranch to ranch, so no one took much note of Elizabeth's book. Chance found some of Whitman's lines familiar, but mostly he had a vague sense of recognition that left him restless.

Toward morning he had one of those dreams that haunt us all through the day. He dreamed he had ridden up-valley with Several to hunt a gigantic lion that was devouring the herd. They separated in the high country, then Chance left his horse in the meadow and climbed on foot into the pass for a look around.

The view of the valley took his breath away. He found a place to sit where he could spend some time taking it in. He leaned back against a rock and rested his arms by his sides. The place was soft and warm.

He looked down and discovered that he was sitting on a stack of calfskins. He realized at once that the place had been sat in before, though by whom he did not know. Then it came to him, as these things do in dreams, that the skins were lion-killed, and then he knew that he had stumbled onto the throne of the Catamount King.

He was suddenly afraid. He looked around, but the cat was not in sight. The pass was an open place with little cover for stalking, so he told himself he was safe for now. But he knew there was peril there, and knew he must not forget.

He turned back toward the valley and the mountains. The valley opened out far below onto a grassy plain that stretched away to disappear into the pale blue of the sky. In other visits to the pass he had not taken the time to notice just how beautiful it was.

But the feeling of peril caressed the pass like a breeze. He felt it in his face, a mountain breeze that carried the scent of juniper and fir, and he could not understand. He liked it there, liked it very much, but something was not right.

He woke with a start. As the breeze and the pass and the valley disappeared, a realization took their place, as clear as the planks above him: the valley of that dream was not Elizabeth's.

He lay on his bunk for perhaps an hour as the morning began to grow light, staring at the planks. The valley had been as real as if he had been there the week before; it was not the vague and fleeting setting of a dream, but a place he had been before. A memory.

52

He lay there trying to bring the memory back, but it had slipped away with the dream. He tried to get back to sleep, but could not. Day had broken anyway and the ranch would soon be coming to life.

He got up and pulled on his clothes and went outside to the privy. When he was finished, he crossed the creek and climbed the hill across from the palace.

He didn't know the meaning of that dream. It was unsettling the way the stories of Toejam Early and Homer Graf had been. But for the first time he knew he wanted to stay.

As he looked down on Elizabeth's ranch, he felt as though he were peering down at his life through the swirling fog in his mind.

He looked around at the morning and watched as Rathead skulked out of the cookhouse and rang the bell for grub.

VIII

THE REGION EAST OF THE RANCH, BETWEEN THE Bighorns and the Powder, was hill country with good grass. The EA kept a line shack in that country, where the men rotated duty keeping the herd out of the river.

Chance topped a hill on the appaloosa one morning and found the shack a short way below in a bowl that also sheltered a pole corral and a spring with a grove of cottonwoods and willows. Two horses stood in the corral, including a buckskin Chance admired. The buckskin belonged to a hand named Bean Bagley, who had ridden out two days earlier. Chance knew Bagley had brought three mounts, so he knew that Bagley was away from the camp.

He tethered his mount at the corral and walked up to the shack, an aging log structure with a cedar roof a little like that of the palace. A firepit hunkering in the dust before the shack supported a half-empty pot of coffee on a wire grill. Chance picked up a cup from a rock by the fire and rinsed it out with a little of the coffee, then poured himself some. He drank a little, then shook his head as if to clear his thoughts and looked into the pot to see if something had crawled into it and died. Finding nothing but coffee, he poured some more and drank it.

A washstand and an old army mirror hung from an oak just beside the front of the cabin. Bagley had made himself comfortable inside but had left a free bunk. After an unhurried lunch, Chance lay down for a nap.

Just as he began to doze off, a man appeared in the door of the shack. He was in his middle twenties with boyish good looks and curly hair that stuck out from his hat, which had been pushed back as if to help him see into the darkened shack. Chance had not heard him coming.

"Gawd dang, Chance," the man said, "you must of had a hard ride. All night, from the look of it." The sun was high, and they were four hours from the ranch.

"Longer'n that," Chance said. "I come out this morning, but seeing you wasn't up yet, I rode back to help Several with a few things, then come out again when the work was done. Glad to see you're up. I'll rustle you some breakfast."

"Amount of work I've did while you've been napping, I'm dang near due for supper."

The men went outside, where Bagley restarted the fire to heat the coffee. They poured cups of the stuff and discussed where they might find cattle.

The coffee was very strong. Cowboys sometimes liked to outdo each other in the department of strong coffee, as they were better known to do in the department of strong whiskey, and spoke of each other's with the vilest contempt.

"Your coffee tastes like lizard piss," they would say, or something of the sort.

"Bull fart," the offender would say, "the stronger the better."

"Of course," they would say, "but this stuff tastes like weasle wizz."

They would go on that way until someone changed the subject: *ad nauseam*, as Virgil might have said.

Most cowboys made their coffee less strong when they were alone; Bagley's was strong because he had known

55

Chance was coming. Moreover, he had made a whole pot of it for breakfast and let it sit over the fire all morning, then had reheated it for lunch instead of making more.

Chance drank some because he needed the help to wake up, then threw the rest into the weeds.

"What's the matter," Bagley said, "no stomach?"

"No, that ain't it—my horse just don't like it when I'm faster than he is."

They spent the afternoon beating the brush up some draws northeast of the cabin. They found a few head, all with good brands.

"Tomorrow we ought to go down and work the river," Bagley said, and Chance agreed. It was always best to work the rivers and bogs in pairs.

When they returned to the shack, they fixed beans and bacon for supper, with plenty of biscuits, which Bagley fried up in the bacon grease. They sat on logs near the fire and ate and drank coffee as the shadows grew long across the hills around them. Chance made the coffee this time, and made it to his own liking.

"*Damn*, this here coffee's weak," Bagley said.

"Yeah. Good, ain't it?"

Bagley winked at Chance and took another sip. "I don't guess I'll throw it in the weeds," he said.

Chance got up and put a couple more logs on the fire. He liked having firewood so close to camp. He had been in a lot of camps where they had burned only cowchips. The problem with the cowchip campfire was that it didn't crackle. A crackling fire cast a spell over a good camp in open country that a cowchip fire simply could not match.

He sat on his log and poked at the fire with a stick. "You worked for the Widder long?" he said.

"About four years."

"Where you from originally?"

56

"Here and there," Bagley said, "wherever there's cows."

"Yes, of course, you're a cowboy ain't you? So where was that?"

Bagley pushed his hat back and squinted into the flames, then squirted a stream of the coffee like tobacco spit between his teeth into the fire. "Nebrasky, I reckon. Seems kinda long ago, now."

"Haw, haw," Chance shouted. "Must have been all of five years ago."

"Waal," Bagley said, "I agree I ain't seen quite the decades you have." He spat a stream of the coffee once more. "What about you?"

"I have to admit," Chance said, "I've been around so long I ain't quite sure where I'm from no more."

"Ain't you from Texas, or what?"

"Yeah, I reckon, or someplace. Wherever it was, it was cow country—sure wasn't no Nebrasky. But tell me, where all have you rode?"

"Nebrasky, of course," Bagley said, "Kansas—rode a little yahoo there—Colorado, little bit up in Montana. But mostly right here."

Chance asked him about Montana, about the Larson and Big Sky spreads, and about the outfit known as Paradise.

"Paradise," Bagley said, scratching his head. "Big Sky. Can't think of 'em, though Larson seems to ring a bell. Why, you looking for someone?"

"Not exactly. Fella in Texas told me once about an outfit he thought I might like, but he was a little vague on the details, so I just keep an ear to the wind, as they say."

"You thinking of moving on?"

"Oh, no. I was for a while, but I've grown kinda partial to this outfit here."

"That's me," Bagley said. "This here's about the best damn country I've ever rode in. And the Widder's a right decent boss, too, you have to admit."

57

"What about her?" Chance said. "I still haven't quite figured her out."

"Well damn, Chance! She made you her top hand, didn't she? I don't reckon you must think too poorly of her."

"No, that ain't what I meant. Sure she's been good to me, and she seems to know the business okay, but she is after all a lady in a man's world. For example, how come she set a new feller like me to top hand over a loyal one like yourself? Wasn't that a little risky? She don't know me that well—drifter like me, she don't even know if I'll stay. And a hand like you that's stuck with her all these years, you might have took offense and just rode off."

"Didn't though, did I?" Bagley said. "It crossed my mind, seeing a new hand get my job, especially an old peckerwood like you—but I figure you won't last forever, and by that time I'll be the mature type myself. Widder seems to prefer maturity in her top rider over pure skill and such."

"So why did you stay?"

"Just what I said. I never worked for no lady before Mr. Allen passed away, and I didn't know how I'd take to it. But she's turned out a damn good boss, and a right handsome one at that, with maybe the finest ranch on earth. A man would be a fool to leave this place. I'm too young for responsibility anyway. I reckon I owe it to the Widder for not forcing it on me before my time."

"Well, you have got loyalty, I'll give you that. How do the other fellas feel about the Widder?"

"Ah, Chancie, Chancie," Bagley said, wagging his finger, "I hope you ain't thinkin' what I think you're a-thinkin'."

"And just what do you think I'm a-thinkin', boy?"

"Well, you see, dang near every hand that ever comes through here falls in love with the Widder sooner or later. I mean, she has a damn sight more of a certain appeal than your average rancher. But sooner or later everybody falls back out of love with her, too. After all, she is the boss and she's older than most of us anyway. Everybody but you and Several. And poor old Several, I don't think he's ever quite fell back out of love. Looks upon her like a daughter, he says. Kind of looks after her like that, too. If you ask me, old Several's purely in love with her, always has been. But he's good for her. He does look after her."

"She don't seem to encourage that sort of thing, though."

"No, hell no. She keeps her distance—with the boys, anyhow. I don't know what she does up there in the palace with Several. Or with you, for that matter."

Chance smiled. "You'll never know, either, boy."

Bagley grinned and squirted into the fire again, only this time with Red Man chaw.

The cabin was too hot for sleeping, so the men threw their bedrolls onto the ground not far from the fire. Chance watched the stars for a while, then listened to Bagley start to snore. Bagley harbored an attachment to the boss that was more than simple cowhand loyalty. Maybe Bagley was in love with her the way he said everyone else was.

Chance thought about Elizabeth. She was unhappy; there was a loneliness in her life she didn't like to show but couldn't quite conceal. Maybe, he thought, men fell in love with Elizabeth's loneliness.

Whatever the reason, Chance had felt the power of Elizabeth's charm, and had even wondered from time to time what she would be like in the great feather bed he imagined she had. He understood that she was part of the reason he was staying. There was no goddamn Larson. There was no goddamn Paradise. He wondered, as he lay under the Wyoming sky, if he could get Elizabeth to like him. That was an absorbing thought. He pictured her in her bed, and liked what he saw. He knew his chances of ever seeing for himself, but he wondered just the same.

He dreamed that night of a man whose face he could not see, a tall old man, an Indian perhaps, or a Mexican. The old man stood at a distance and watched, and seemed to want Chance to approach, though he said nothing. Chance woke from that dream in a hard sweat and got up and climbed the hill above the shack and watched the night until he grew tired enough once more to sleep.

IX

IF THERE IS NO GOD, DOSTOYEVSKY SUGGESTED, everything is permitted. Anything goes. And anything may be possible. Yet even if God does exist, as the Twentieth Century learned, just about anything is possible anyway.

The men got up early and rode east toward the river. Chance watched the shape of the land as they rode. This was their winter range; he wanted to know the lay of the gullies and the slopes as well as he could before they were covered with snow.

They gathered a few head on the way to the river and drifted them back toward the shack. After an hour or so they started down a rocky draw to the river.

Near the bottom of the draw they picked up the scent of wood smoke among the rocks.

"Looks like we're company," Bagley said.

"Good. Maybe there's food."

They rounded a rocky bluff to their right and came out on a flood plain beside the river. A small campfire smoldered under a battered coffeepot. Three hobbled horses grazed nearby. The men got down and helped themselves to coffee from the pot using cups they found in the camp.

"Damn," Bagley said, "this coffee tastes like buzzard shit."

61

"Tastes like yours," Chance said, and took a long swallow.

"Mine! Oh, mine has a kick to it, sure, but this here is plain vulture dump."

They finished the coffee, then mounted and started upstream past the camp. In about half a mile they came upon a crew from an outfit known as the Hook and Ring.

The Hook and Ring hands were towing a steer from the river. The animal was stuck halfway up to its knees in mud just under the shallows at the edge of the stream, but did not appear to appreciate the efforts of the men.

The moment the steer was free of the mire, it charged one of the riders. The man roared some profanities and nearly went down. "Dammit, Flynn," he shouted, "I told you we ought to put two ropes on this beast."

The beast, now trailing the rider's rope from his horns, trotted a few yards up the riverbed, then stopped and turned back. He looked over the army of men and horses assembled by the river, then turned again and trotted away up the river.

"EA stock," Bagley said. "Don't worry about your rope. We'll need it to drag him out of the bog again anyway—we'll get it back for you then."

The man called Flynn introduced himself to Chance and Bagley, then introduced them to the others. The one introduced as Murphy was still recovering from his brush with the steer, and from losing his rope.

"Seems to me we're risking our necks saving everybody's beeves but our own," he said.

"Not to mention our ropes and all," Flynn said.

"I've done enough cow saving for now," Murphy grumbled. "Let's get back to camp. My nerves could use a shot of that coffee."

They went back to the camp and put more coffee on the fire. They talked a while about the cattle and drank the coffee, then as the Hook and Ring men broke camp, Chance and Bagley started up the river to finish the work the others had begun.

About a mile upstream they came upon the steer that had taken Murphy's rope. Just as Bagley had predicted, the animal was mired again.

"I reckon he's about fit to be hung with that there rope," Bagley said.

They towed the animal from the bog, and as soon as the steer was free Chance roped him by the hind legs and brought him down, so that Bagley could retrieve Murphy's rope.

Later the men chased that steer up a draw and back to the safety of higher ground.

When they returned to camp, the Hook and Ring hands had already arrived. They had mustered their cattle and moved them to a bowl north of the shack.

"Come on down and set a spell," Flynn told them. "Accommodations ain't too good, but the grub sets well enough."

"You, Murphy," Bagley said. "I reckon this here's your rope." He held out Murphy's rope, neatly coiled, and everyone laughed. "I found it wrapped around the horns of an old bearkiller over yonder," Bagley said. "He didn't want to give it up, but I said, 'Hell, it's Murphy's rope, ain't it?' so he forked it over."

Murphy scratched his head as Bagley handed him the rope. Everyone had a good laugh as Bagley and Chance turned their horses in at the corral.

One of the men had shot a pronghorn on the way back from the river. The men hacked slabs of meat from the carcass and broiled them over the fire. Murphy and Bagley traded gibes the whole time, and kept the others laughing so hard they could hardly eat.

"Old Murphy walked into this saloon," Bagley said, "and he was wearing a chicken on his head."

"A chicken!" the men shouted. "Haw, haw . . . "

The men laughed at Bagley's story, but Murphy was not to be outdone. "Why, that ain't nothin',," he said. "I run into Bagley in Casper one time when he was just coming off a trail drive and had this unbearable itch to get himself . . . "

And so on, *ad absurdum.*

The stories ran to women, as they usually did in places like that.

"How many of you have ever met up with Calamity Jane?" Murphy said. No one had.

Murphy spoke effusively of the legendary Calamity, whom he said he had bedded in Montana, where she was known as the queen of the scarlet doves. He talked about going back to Montana for another whack.

"I don't know," Flynn said. "Only Calamity Jane I ever heard of was six foot tall and wore men's duds and was said to be as good as any man with whiskey, chaw, or rawhide whip. First cousin to the Grizzly, what I heard."

"Takes a gal with a little spitfire in her to survive them Montana winters," Murphy grinned. "That's the way we like 'em there."

The men had another good laugh at Murphy about his taste for "hellroaring Montana tomcats." Murphy was Montana bred; he had grown up and worked around Miles City. As much from curiosity as anything, Chance asked him the once inevitable questions.

"Everybody in Montana knows that story," Murphy said. "Kind of a legend in them parts. Still some sort of hysteria going on up there, too—or so I heard. But I reckon the Paradise outfit itself is long gone."

They sat around the fire and spun yarns till after dark. Chance listened to Murphy's Montana stories with an unexpected detachment; they cracked no lightning now, pealed no thunder.

Montana was only a few days' ride away, but seemed as

64

far now as it had once seemed to him in Texas. Chance watched the dying fire and listened to the tall talk and thought about the Widder. She was near. She was real.

The men left the fire and crawled into their blankets. Chance studied the stars as he had on so many nights before, and thought about the Widder.

One of the men snickered from his blankets. "A chicken on his head," he said.

Then they were asleep.

WHEN CHANCE AND BAGLEY RETURNED TO THE ranch, they returned to bad news. Several was dead. Dust to dust. His horse had thrown him for a loop. Several had said they were both getting too old for real work, and now he lay in the icehouse waiting to be buried.

Chance went up to the palace to see Elizabeth. She looked older, and very tired. Dark shades stained the skin below her eyes. She didn't appear to have been crying, but Chance thought it might have been better if she had.

She planned to bury Several on the hill behind the palace. Suffering Pete had been sent to Crazywoman for the Lutheran pastor. Elizabeth spoke well of the pastor and said there was no one she would rather have bury her friend. He was expected to come the next day with a box; no one on the ranch wanted to build the box.

As Chance started for the door, Elizabeth seemed to hold back.

"Chance," she said. Her eyes were filled with pain as they scanned his face. "Make sure he's okay, will you? Make sure he's safe?"

"Of course," he said.

She held back still, and Chance could see that she

didn't want him to go. Bernadetta had been away for several days, and Elizabeth had no one even to talk to. He knew this was a terrible time for her to be alone—but he didn't know what to say.

"I . . . " he said, and looked at his hands. "I'll take care of him."

As he turned to leave, Elizabeth blocked his retreat for just a moment before letting him go. She touched his hand and looked into his eyes, then he fled into the night.

Nobody played cards in the bunkhouse that night. Nobody told stories. And nobody talked about Several. A few of the men wrote letters or read, but others just turned in early. Chance turned in.

He found himself thinking more about Elizabeth than Several. She had surprised him when she touched his hand. He thought about the look in her eyes, and saw that she had been asking him to stay with her for a while. He thought about her alone in that house with her grief, and wished he had stayed.

But he thought about Several as well, the only man in the world beside Toejam Early who knew about him. Now they were both gone, he was sure, and he was alone too. He thought about Elizabeth again, and wished again that he had stayed.

In the morning a couple of the hands dug a grave up on the hill. The pastor arrived about noon, a balding athletic man with a square jaw and wire-rim glasses. His arrival raised everybody's spirits, and Elizabeth especially seemed to feel better. Chance understood why she had wanted him to come.

The funeral was short. As soon as Several was in the ground the pastor left, and Elizabeth invited everyone to the palace. She had risen early to cook for them, and the

67

men attacked the food with their customary zeal.

And Elizabeth served them brandy. Chance nearly took one, just a short one for Several, but he recognized at once how much he wanted that drink. He fought off the sweat that came up on his face, and settled for coffee with his pie.

Elizabeth looked much better now, and Chance felt she would be all right. He left with the other men. She did not touch him this time, did not look into his eyes. She was the boss again, and her ranch was on the mend.

The following morning Elizabeth came to the cookhouse and asked Chance to see her at the palace as soon as breakfast was done. When he came up the hill she showed him into her office, a large study with leather furniture and bookcases to the ceiling.

"Thank you for your help," she said. "I'm going to miss him. He was a good friend." She looked away a moment, then back. "And a good ramrod. I needed him here. I won't be able to replace him."

"No," he said, "I reckon not."

"But I've got to have a foreman," she said. "Chance, I'd like you to be my foreman. It will pay an extra fifteen a month and you can have Several's cabin. What do you say?"

He made a fist and blew into it. "I guess I was planning to stay anyway. I was going to tell Several. I don't reckon it will be quite the same without the old crank, but I'd be honored to have his job."

Her eyes lit up and she shook his hand. "Thank you. I'll tell the men. I'm also thinking of making Bagley top hand. What do you think?"

"A good boy. He'll do."

"You can tell him after I've told the hands about you. I'll help you clean out the cabin before you move in. I want to . . . I don't know. I want to take care of Several's things." Tears came to her eyes. "He was a good man, Chance," she said. Then she smiled a little. "I'll meet with the men in the bunkhouse in ten minutes. Better let them know."

Chance told the men the Widder was coming. They took their underwear down from hooks and clotheslines around the place.

Elizabeth came down and explained about Chance's new job. She told the men they could divide Several's property after she and Chance had taken out a few things. Then Chance made some adjustments in the job assignments and sent the men to work.

Several's cabin was small but nicely furnished, with an oval rug and an old oak rocking chair and a rolltop desk. A dark sea chest sat against the wall at the foot of the bed.

Chance piled Several's clothes on the bed, then sat down and watched for a few moments as Elizabeth went through the desk. She was so absorbed she did not seem to notice. She was wearing men's clothing, the dungaree pants and green suspenders and flannel shirt she often wore when she worked on the ranch. Chance remembered what Flynn had said about Calamity Jane, but didn't think the comparison held.

Elizabeth looked good in her men's clothing as she pondered the things she found in Several's desk. Most of the things were papers relating to the ranch; Several had played a hand in running the business as well as managing the men. But there were personal things, too. In a drawer Elizabeth found a bundle of letters. They were not letters about the ranch.

"I'm going to keep these," she said, turning to Chance. She held the bundle in her hand and looked from it to him and back again. "These letters are old. He had no kin. His only friends were here in these parts. These letters are a part of Several I never knew."

She looked at Chance a little the way she had looked at

him before, in her house the night Several had died. "I can't just throw them away," she said. "I won't ever read them, I have no right. But I guess I'll keep them. Maybe that's something I can do for him now."

She turned away and busied herself with the other things in the desk. Chance watched her a little longer. She looked comical in those clothes, yet she wore them and carried herself with a grace that seemed to hold him in a spell. When he came at last to his senses, he got up and looked around for something else to do.

"Maybe I should go through the chest," he said.

"Thank you," was all she said.

He opened the chest and began to remove the contents, placing the things on Several's bed. Among them were two more packets of letters. He crossed to the desk and gave the letters to Elizabeth. He saw that she was struggling not to cry.

"I'm sorry," he said. "I'll go tend the horses."

"No," she said, smiling a little, "don't go, I'm okay." She looked down for a second, then put something she was holding on the desk. "I'd like you to get moved in this morning. I have some things I want to go over with you this afternoon."

She told him to keep the chest and the blankets and to give the rest of the things to the men. He stacked up the usable clothing and carried it to the bunkhouse, where he left it on his vacant bunk. Then he returned to the cabin.

Elizabeth had packed various things in a crate.

"Let's go up to the office now and get that out of the way," she said. "You can use the afternoon to get settled."

He carried the crate up to the palace and set it in the parlor. Bernadetta had returned, and Elizabeth asked her to make lunch. Then Elizabeth and Chance went to her office, where she taught him some of the ways of turning cows into money.

70

The lunch was something Chance did not recognize served between slices of bread. Sandwiches. They were good with coffee.

"All this reminds me of the time after Richard died," Elizabeth said. "I was very confused. I had come to Wyoming with him, and I had to decide whether to go back to Pennsylvania or to stay. I loved it here, but just then I hated it, too." She laughed at herself for a moment, remembering that time, and shook her head. "I really didn't know what to do."

"What made you decide to stay?"

"I loved it here—and I still do. There were some legal matters, mostly back east, but I had lawyers to settle those. The ranch is part of me. I built it as much as Richard did—except for this crazy chateau. He had the house built almost as soon as we arrived, then gave it to me as an anniversary gift. He actually dreamt of building this ranch into an empire, and wanted a house that looked like some sort of Greco-Roman citadel. I rather like the irony of that; the one part of this ranch that has never really been mine is the part he gave me. The rest was as much mine as his. I couldn't leave it. For what? There was nothing for me in Pennsylvania. And Several was here. He was very loyal—he made it much easier to stay."

"How did your husband die—do you mind my asking?"

Elizabeth held her cup just off the table and began to move it in little circles so the coffee swirled inside the cup. She watched it intently, as if her memory of her husband were clearest for her somewhere down in the eddy of the coffee. When she looked up, Chance could see that she was struggling with this. "He went to Connecticut on business," she said, "and . . . died. That was the end of Richard and his dreams. His family buried him there. That was the end of everything."

She began to swirl her coffee again and watch it with the same intensity she had shown a moment before.

71

He studied this woman's face as she studied her coffee, apparently unaware once more of his presence in her world. He studied her face and her hands and her arms. Though she was not beautiful by most standards, he had always found her attractive. Now he began to find her beautiful as well.

Her face was an assemblage of faintly uneven parts—her nose, her mouth, even her chin lacked the symmetry he associated with beauty. And he noticed for the first time that she even had a few freckles.

Yet her face was more beautiful than the sum of those parts. It was a strong face yet a soft face, a good face. The tilt of her head, the slope of her nose, the steadiness of those brown eyes were lovely, and revealed, he thought, a good heart. But it was an expressive face, too, and it expressed something just then that Chance did not think he understood.

He looked at her hands. They were strong, too, like her face, though not as soft, but Chance liked them as well. They were good hands; they were real. He wanted to be touched by those hands.

Chance felt himself being drawn into the eddy of Elizabeth's beauty as she was drawn into the swirling in her cup.

She looked up from her coffee and found him watching her there in her Wyoming palace.

"Well," she said. "Hello. I believe I was away for a moment."

"That's okay," he said. "The place was in good hands."

"I think it was," she said. "Thanks again."

XI

THE SANDWICH ENTERED HISTORY ABOUT A hundred years before the life of Ebenezer Chance. It was named for the English nobleman who first recognized that slices of bread with layers of baloney sausage between them were in some way analogous to the universe in which we live.

Chance spent the afternoon settling in at the cabin and looking over the work on his new desk. Elizabeth wanted him to learn the business of the ranch as well as he knew the herding of the cattle.

He ate supper with the hands in the grubhouse. They needled him about his new job, and Bagley even worse.

He spent the evening in his cabin thinking about the Widder. He started to go over some figures he had looked at in the afternoon, but couldn't keep his mind on the figures; another figure kept coming to mind. He got out a book of the poetry Elizabeth had given him from her library, but his mind was not on poetry any more than numbers. He thought about going back up to the bunkhouse to play cards with the others—but that wasn't what he wanted either.

What he wanted was to think about Elizabeth. He wanted to think about her face and her hands, about her lovely shape, and about the good heart and the deep loneliness she had dared to let him see.

He lay down on the bunk, so recently that of his friend, and let himself think. He let himself think about Elizabeth, and he let himself think about the feelings that clamored like neuropathic revolutionaries in the boulevards of his mind. He wondered if he had ever had feelings like those before.

In any event, he had them now, and they would not leave him. He kept seeing Elizabeth: as he had first seen her in roundup camp, as he had found her grieving one evening, as he had looked her over from that very spot just that morning, and as he had watched her, lost in her coffee and her memories, in her palace that afternoon. He wished now, more than ever, that he had stayed with her the night he had left her with her grief. He wanted to be with her now, to know what she was feeling, to be certain she was okay, to share her sorrow and make her laugh—and to make her feel about him the way he felt about her.

Elizabeth no longer seemed beyond his reach. She liked him, he knew, and had already reached out to him once. He also knew that his appearance, for which men teased him, was not disliked by women; if anything, it seemed to captivate them. As poorly favored as it was, perhaps, it was something other men did not have. He wondered if his appearance captivated the boss.

Chance's excitement centers were humming now. He got up and paced the floor. He thought for a moment about the fantasy that had brought him to Wyoming, and about Montana, for which he had been bound, and felt the fog curling through the dark recesses of his brain. The fog: that goddamned fog. But his excitement centers were humming now.

He went up to the bunkhouse. Bagley and Willaree

74

were playing stud poker for quarters and were glad to have another hand. That night Chance made bankrupts of them both.

Chance had dinner with Elizabeth in her palace every Monday evening. They talked about ranching, but often talked into the evening about poetry and history and even politics.

She also began to tell him more about herself. She had planned to be a school mistress until she met Richard Allen and moved to Wyoming to ranch. Richard was a college man who had taken up the law at Yale but left law school to pursue what seemed a crazy dream of becoming a cattle baron, scarcely acknowledging that the day of cattle barony in the West was gone.

Elizabeth had met Richard at a ladies' weekend at Yale and was swept away by his charm and his dreams. At first his talk of the West had seemed amusing, but the more she saw of him, the more she saw that he had convinced himself of the possibility of the thing.

She married him as much from fascination as love, and embarked with him on his adventure. The house was part of Richard's dream, the palace with its command of his domain, so well made it could have withstood cannonfire. It was visible for miles to the east and south, and looked like no other ranch house in five states. Richard had been obsessed with it, as if raising his palace on that hill might grant legitimacy to his dream and inevitability to his empire.

As Elizabeth told all this to Chance, that look he had seen before crept into her face, and something like it into her voice. Part of her had loved the dream too, and that love had kept her there—but there was part of her, as well, that was weary of a dream that had lost so much of its charm.

The weariness in her face was clear, and betrayed some heaviness, some hurt she carried inside for something deeper than the tarnishing of the dream.

But it didn't dwell in her face for long. In speaking of Richard and herself, she had led Chance, at last, back to something she had been working toward all along.

"Well," she said. "I've told you everything there is to know about me, but I still don't know a thing about you."

"Sure you do," he said.

"And what is that?"

"I reckon you already know I ain't either a drinking man or a Mormon."

"Ah, but what I don't reckon I know is how you came to that blissful condition."

Chance knew she had him. And he knew that this time she wasn't going to let him go.

"That there is something of a story," he said.

"That's good," she said. "I love stories."

Chance inhaled, then cleared his throat. The time had come.

"Okay," he said.

He blew a long, slow breath into his fist, then told her about the morning he had found his memory gone.

"Amnesia," she said, a note of wonder in her voice.

"I reckon," he said. "Amnesia. Guardian spirit of the lost forgetful."

"Yes," she laughed, "maybe so."

"I don't guess I've found her in the literature, but I know her well enough, all right. I expect she's the one that brought me to Wyoming."

"So what became of your memory? Do you have any idea?"

"Nope," he said. "The whole thing is a puzzle. I can remember Virgil and Homer just fine, but I can't remember my own name."

"What about 'Chance'?"

"Came to me at random," he said.

Elizabeth laughed. "Well then," she said, "what *do* you remember?"

"About myself? Nothing before waking up with the horrors one day in jail, except a little about lolling in the dirt watching the sun come up and the prairie spin around my head." He told her nothing about Toejam or the story that had captured his imagination.

Elizabeth drew her hands up before her and rested her arms on the edge of the table while she brought the tips of her fingers together. "Well," she said once more.

She watched him for a moment as if she might see inside him to find his other name, then let a sly smile steal across her face. He thought how funny it was that he had not noticed those freckles sooner.

"So," she said, "you are something of a mystery after all."

His spirit soared: she was interested. He smiled a little timidly and looked down at the table.

"Yes ma'm," he said. "So it seems."

In September Bagley came down from the valley and reported some new kills. Chance decided to have another look for himself.

After a breakfast of bacon and eggs and fairly decent coffee, he started up the valley on the appaloosa. The morning was still young, and the breeze had a nip Chance had not felt all summer. The air was sweet and clear and bore the hint of something he had smelled before, though he couldn't have told you when or where.

He counted a few head of cattle in the woods along the valley, but most had wandered into the higher country up the two forks of the stream.

He found two kills in the meadow where he and Several had staked out the calf. Both were old. He decided not to try the calf trick again, and threw his bedroll down in the meadow.

In the morning he ate a couple of biscuits and started up the pass on foot. The air was sharp, but warmed quickly in the sun. In the flat of the pass he found a cat track in the sand.

He looked around. To the west, down a long canyon and beyond another ridge, lay the valley of the Big Horn. He filled his lungs with that thin air once more: oxygen, the sweetest he could remember.

He looked east across the EA ranch and began to sense what the country would be like with the changing of the seasons. Within a week or two new snow would dust the mountaintops. The nights would grow colder, though the days would stay warm into October. There on the pass the breeze, even on warm days, would carry the scent of winter coming. In the bottom at the mouth of the canyon the aspen would turn yellow, but there on the higher slopes the larches would turn the brightest gold. The larches. Against the blue of the October sky and the white of new snow the larches would dazzle beyond anything else he could recall.

He was remembering. He had been in autumn mountains before. He didn't know when or where—but he was remembering.

He lay down and stretched himself out on his back in the sun and watched the sky, not quite trying to see the past any more but still holding that possibility like a shot of good whiskey in the back of his mind. A redtailed hawk was riding an updraft above him, circling as it rose slowly, slowly into the sky. He watched it circle for five or ten minutes, growing smaller and smaller as it climbed. Suddenly, as it came around the arc of a spiral, it caught some unseen windstream in the sky and sped away at an unbelievable speed toward the south.

Chance sat up and watched the hawk until it became the merest speck in the sky. Then it was gone. He strained to make it out once more, but could see nothing now but the blue of the sky. He stood up and looked out across the country one more time, then started down the pass to get his horse.

XII

FALL ROUNDUP WAS THE KIND OF WORK COW-hands live for. Six men beat the two forks of the valley for a week and drove the cattle down to winter range, while four or five others worked along the foot of the mountains collecting livestock fugitives there.

With autumn settling onto the ranch, Chance returned to the high country and found it the way he remembered. And soon the aspen along the creek above the bunk-house turned as he knew they would.

On cold mornings he sometimes skipped eating with the men in order to watch the sunrise and feel the rhythms of the earth as they could only be felt just then. Hoarfrost dusted the yellow leaves and grew in needles from the ground. A fine stillness hung in the air as smoke from the cookhouse tinged the morning with its scent. And over it all, strong and outlandish and elegant, brooded the palace.

Another memory tarried here, Chance was sure: the dawn had always been his favorite time.

Winter descended in November amidst a chaos of gray and white. Winter in the town of Casper had been a dull and bitter affair, but on the EA it had a vigor Chance liked.

He liked riding out into the cold; he even liked the wind, though he cursed it.

He took his turn riding line. In bad weather the range could be harsh and deadly, but on clear days it was beautiful. Chance loved it when stormy weather broke and the sun or the stars blazed through the wildness of the sky and the blowing snow.

The nights he spent at the ranch were usually passed playing cards with the men or reading in his cabin or having dinner with the boss.

His feelings for Elizabeth had pacified themselves, but only a little. He was drawn to her at least in part by that unspoken mystery of her own, that ghost or suffering she did not easily show, drawn to her as if, in plumbing the depths of her mystery, he might learn something about his.

Elizabeth did not seem to be aware of his interest. She seemed to like his company, and from time to time she even showed a certain fondness—but she maintained a reserve that reminded him always who was the employer and who the hired hand.

One evening their talk turned to politics. Elizabeth was pleased to have a rancher in the White House, especially a literate one. "That four-eyed cowboy," she called him. "Do you realize that he is the first American President of the Twentieth Century?"

"What about McKinley?"

"Oh, he doesn't count," she said. "I think it's funny that the cowboy is really the first Twentieth Century President. Don't you find it exciting to belong to a new century?"

"I don't remember the old one," he said.

"The world is changing so fast it makes me giddy. The horseless carriage and the telephone and the electric light weren't enough. Now they have a wireless device that can send messages across the Atlantic, and I just read that they have developed a flying machine."

81

"And you think these things will change the world?"

"My stars, Chance, what do you think? If this flying thing follows the same course as the electrical inventions, we'll be talking and flying all over the earth. Nothing will ever be the same, and we're on the brink of it all right now."

"From the top of my bronc it don't look much different to me," he said.

She laughed. "Try sitting face forward. History is accelerating toward its destiny, Chance, and we are witnessing this in our own time. Better get on board while you can."

"I haven't gotten over my fascination with the past just yet," he said.

"Well, this is the West, my friend. We have no past here, only future—and the future depends on us. Look to the future. It will teach you more than memory ever could."

Elizabeth was toying with him. He didn't know whether she was talking more about civilization or about him.

"Waal, to the future, then," he said, hoisting his mug, "though I am still wondering how we got where we are."

She looked into her cup again as she always seemed to do when she was thinking about something, then picked it up and swirled it once or twice.

She looked up. "What's important to you?" she said.

"To me?" he said, searching his thoughts. "Funny you ask. I've been puzzling over that myself of late."

"I don't mean whatever may have been important to you once, but right now, as the man you are today with a year of past and a pretty real present, I think, and a future that is pure possibility."

Chance laughed out loud. "Possibility," he said.

"But you're a very real fellow, Chance, if you don't mind my saying. Whatever your past *or* your future, something must be important to you. Tell me what it is. Do you know?"

"I've studied on the past and the future until I've about

wore myself out with them, but I suppose the thing that means the most is being here doing what I'm doing."

"I'm glad to hear that," she said, "but I'll be out of books before long, then maybe things will change. How will I keep you here then to run my outfit?"

"Oh, it would take a lot to separate me from the EA, though running out of books would be a substantial change. Of course," he added, "you could raise my pay. Then I could send for more books."

"Raise your pay!" she said. "You don't earn what I pay you now, always off riding line like some rawhide rangehand."

"Ah, you'll never keep me from riding the range, boss. That's the one thing I know I've always done—the part of my past that decides the future for sure."

"Then tell me, Mr. Chance, what was it that brought you riding up the range from Texas to Carthage-by-the-Bighorns?"

"From Texas," he said. "Pretty much of an abstraction, I suppose."

He told her about the old man in Texas and what the old man had told him, and how the dream of a lost birthright had given him a reason to live again and had brought him north in search of the imponderable Larson.

"I can understand why you didn't want to tell me this before," she said.

"I reckon you could have let me go. I'm glad you didn't."

"So am I," she said. "I thought about it, but Several asked me to keep you. That old puddinghead, I never could trust his judgment."

He saw a flicker of sorrow in her eyes. Elizabeth looked down at her cup again. When she looked up, the flicker was gone.

"So you wandered from Texas to Wyoming in search of the golden fleece," she said.

"I guess that pretty well says it."

"But then you stayed. Why?"

"Well, first of all, because the same old puddinghead talked to me."

"He had a way of doing that, didn't he?"

"Seems he did. He thought I should take a look at what I had here and decide which was worth more. So I took that look, and I guess I liked what I saw—the ranch, the operation, the old puddinghead . . ." He looked at his hands for a moment, then looked up at Elizabeth. "Even the boss," he said.

Elizabeth tugged a corner of her lower lip back under two or three of her teeth for a moment, then reached out and put her hand on his.

"She is something of an enchantress, you know," she said.

"And she got me to stay on through the winter."

Elizabeth took her hand from his. "So she did. And so, will you be leaving in the spring after all?"

Chance looked into her face to see what it might tell him at just that moment. It was hard to read. He looked at his hands for a moment while he tried to think of the truth.

"No," he said.

"Then what has become of this dream of yours? Have you really decided to bury the past and start again?"

"That dream was the hankering of a frightened man. It served a purpose, I guess—it gave him hope. And it brought him here. It may even be true, I don't know, but I'm not sure I want to go on dividing myself between living and chasing phantoms."

She put her hand on his again and looked into his eyes. "Will you stay, then? Can I count on you?"

He took her hand in his and held it, and saw something in her eyes he had not seen before. "Yes," he said.

He stood up, still holding her hand, and brought her to

84

her feet, and they moved silently toward each other and embraced. And then they kissed, a good kiss, a long kiss that set his excitement centers buzzing and snapping almost beyond belief.

"I love you," she said, looking into his eyes again.

"Me too," he said, and they kissed again.

They did not rush to her bed. Chance wanted Elizabeth very much, but he loved her and wanted for her sake to be sure of her love for him. In the days that followed, much of her reserve seemed to melt, even though she was still the boss, but she was in no hurry to give herself away.

Yet there is a time to embrace, and when the time came it was different for Chance than any other time. He loved her.

She hadn't made love since Richard died, she said, but she didn't seem to have forgotten a thing. She was beautiful in her bed, and she touched him with those beautiful hands, and was as real as she was warm. They mingled their juices and shared the beauty of each other late into the night and deep into the starry universe. She touched his face with tenderness and wonder and looked into his eyes with that look he had seen before.

"That day was the first cause of death," Virgil had written of other lovers, "and first of sorrow." But Chance, like love, was blind. He saw only that this beautiful woman loved him, and his spirit soared and soared.

XIII

THE SKY PROMISED MORE SNOW AND LET DOWN A cold gray light that flattened the features of the land. Even that light was beginning to dim.

The snow on the slope came up to the appaloosa's knees. "Yoooou, Horse," Chance said softly, and let the horse find the way down.

Smoke curled from the shack and Bagley's buckskin stood in the corral. Bean himself came to the door when he heard the horses. Chance took the appaloosa to the corral and waded through the snow to the shack.

"What's for eats?" he asked.

Bagley gestured to a pot on the stove. "What else?" he said.

"Got enough for two?"

"I got me enough beans for the entire Cheyenne nation, if need be," he said. "I figured you'd be along one of these days."

"Well, I ain't no Cheyenne nation, but if you've got the beans, Pardner, I've got the time."

The beans were good, with big hunks of bacon, and the coffee was fresh. "Mm," Chance said of the beans. "Nitrogen. Builds strong bones."

Bagley snickered. "That what it does?"

"That's right," Chance said as he refilled his face. "Nitrogen. Couldn't live without it."

Bagley snickered again. "Can't always live with it too good, either," he said.

"So where's the herd?" Chance said, sopping up bean sauce with a piece of biscuit.

"Down at the river, where they usually are. Worst of it is, they're pretty well grazed out down there. Me and Sufferin' run them all up out of there a couple weeks ago, but the weather's drove them all back and they're getting hungry. I've ran some of them back up onto high ground, but there's still a pretty good bunch down there."

"I've got Sufferin' and Tinker down at the other shack," Chance said, "so these are all we have to worry about. You reckon we can get them all up onto grass tomorrow?"

"If it don't snow again."

"I ain't ever seen so much snow," Chance said. "Is it always like this around here?"

"Aw, there's been a little winter, but I've seen worse."

Bagley draped himself across his bunk. Chance was sitting in the shack's only chair, a rickety straightback barely big enough to hold his weight. He took tobacco and paper from his shirt pocket and tilted his chair.

"Riding up here this afternoon," Chance said, "I thought of Xenophon and his army struggling upcountry in the snow. You know that story?"

"Who?" Bagley said with a grin. "Guess not, but you know how I love a yarn."

"This one really happened. Couple thousand years ago."

Bagley sat up. "Couple thousand years ago! I know you've been around a while, but how did you stumble onto this one?"

"Oh, just the way you stumble onto anything. Lay on back, and I'll tell you."

87

Chance told him the story of Xenophon and the army of ten thousand Greeks whose stock foundered in the snow until some villagers showed them how to tie hides to the horses' hooves.

"Gawd dang," Bagley said. "And that's a true story that happened thousands of years ago?"

"Sure is," Chance said, "and I'm thinking we may have to tie hides to our own hosshooves before this week is out."

"Gawd dang," Bagley said, scratching his head, "you do know the damndest things."

The men worked hard the next day, though they didn't have to tie hides to their horses' hooves. As they were finishing their beans and bacon that night, Bagley asked Chance if he knew any more stories.

"Know any more of them yarns?" he said.

"Of course," Chance said. "I don't know nothing if I don't know yarns. I'll tell you another true one. This one happened even before the days of Xenophon."

"Gawd dang, Chance. You're makin them up, I know it."

"No no. I find 'em in books, son—true as the day is long. You just set back and see if I'm making this up."

Bagley spread himself across his bunk, as he had the night before, and Chance took up his position in the chair.

"I expect you've heard of the Trojan War?" Chance said.

"That the one where they built this here wooden horse big enough to sneak some fellers inside the gate?"

"That's the one. Well you see, when the war was over and the Trojans had lost, one of the Trojan captains lit out with his men in ships for parts unknown. Now, the god Jupiter had sent him a message that he was to git hisself across the sea to a foreign land called Italy, which hardly anybody had heard of in them days, and this feller Aeneas was to build a mighty city there and dedicate it to Jupiter for saving his buttocks from the Greeks."

Bagley got up. "Sounds like this might be a good long one," he said with his usual grin. He put a couple sticks of wood into the fire, then returned to his bunk.

"So this feller Aeneas set off across the sea, like he was told," Chance said, "but after seven years of mishaps his ships were finally scattered by a storm and blown ashore in Africa, a good long way from Italy.

"This was a desperate state for the Trojans because of Africa being a place of wilderness and desert, so the chance of fixing their ships and getting the hell out of there didn't look too good. But they found a city nearby, called Carthage, run by a queen who had come from a place not far from where the Trojans were from." Chance leaned back and fished the makings from a pocket. He rolled a cigarette, then found a match in his shirt pocket and lit up.

"Now, the name of this here queen was Dido . . ."

Bagley raised his head. "What the hell kind of name is that?"

"Well, it's one of them Trojan kind of names, Bean. What the hell kind of name is Aeneas? It's just the kind of names they had in them days. Listen up, now, and let me do the tellin'.

"This Dido, she had heard of Aeneas because of his fame in the Trojan War and the adventures he and his men had survived in their seven years at sea, and she was impressed to have this very feller at her doorstep.

"Now, you got to understand that Queen Dido was a widder woman. Her husband was murdered by his brother and she had fled with her followers to this god-forsaken land—so a brave, handsome feller like Aeneas looked pretty good to her about then.

"Wellsir, being as Aeneas himself was single at the time, and this Dido was one fine-looking specimen, they took and fell in love. One day while they was out riding, they were trapped in a cave by a thunderstorm, just the two of

89

them, so they used the occasion to . . . ah . . . get married, if you follow my drift."

Bagley raised up off his bunk again. "Why, no, Chancie," he said, "I don't reckon I do. Maybe you could explain it in better detail."

"I don't guess you'd understand it if I did. You just follow along and you'll see where this is going.

"So old Aeneas settled in with Dido and helped her build up the great city of Carthage out of the African desert. But one night Mercury, the messenger of the gods, come to him with a message from Jupiter hisself, and what it said was, 'I thought I told you to get your scrawny self up to Italy and found me a city of my own.'"

Bagley sat up on the edge of the bunk. "Getting kinda hot in here," he said. He got up and opened the door a crack, then returned to his bunk. Chance took a last drag from his handmade, then stuffed it out in an oystershell that had somehow found its way to Wyoming.

"Anyhow," Chance said, "Aeneas, he put up a pretty good argument, but in the end Jupiter was the god and Aeneas wasn't, so he seen which side of the loaf had the bacon.

"When he told Dido that Jupiter had told him to get moving, she like to been hog-tied. But he had to go. He hated to leave—he had the best life going for him he ever had, a beautiful wife and all the wealth and power in that part of the world. But a command from heaven is a command from the top, ain't it? He didn't have much say.

"So Aeneas and his men slipped away to sea one night without even saying adios. When Dido saw that his ships were gone, she ordered a funeral fire to be built. Nobody knew who had died, but they did what they was told. When they had it ready to go, the Queen mounted the logs herself, then ordered the men to set it afire. As the flames climbed toward her, the most beautiful woman in the world, she took Aeneas' sword out of her skirts, on ac-

90

count of he had left it behind, see, and she drove it into her heart."

"Aw, *damn*, Chance."

"It's true. Feller named Virgil wrote it all down. After she fell, the flames come up the pile and grew so tall they could be seen from halfway across the sea. And Dido was gone. Nary a lick of nitrogen left."

"Damn, man. That ain't right."

"Shore it is, Bean. I told you—the feller wrote er all down."

"No, no, I mean what that Trojan feller done. To leave his woman like that."

"Well he had to, Bean! It wasn't like he done it on a whim. When the god orders you to git, I reckon git is what you do."

"Nosir. What god would ever tell a man to betray his woman? That's what it was—betrayal. I met a feller once told me a story about the unforgivable sin. He said there's only one sin in the world the Lord God will never forgive. He never said what that sin was, he just told me to think on it. Well, I done that, and what I come up with clear as day was the sin of betrayal."

"I'll be damn, Bean, that's halfway thoughtful."

"See, here's what betrayal is—it's any time you break a trust. Trust is sacred, see, so I'd say breaking a trust is the unforgivable sin, and that's what we have here, clear as a bell. This here is just a fact: if it was up to me, any man that would break a trust that way could go straight to hell."

"Well I be damn. For a feller of your tender years, you're a deep one, ain't you?

Chance went outside to relieve himself before turning in. He waded through a drift to a place a little distance from the shack that had not been used for the purpose. He enjoyed peeing into the snow, loved the primal thrill of standing alone in the bitter cold carefully wizzing a round hole in-

91

to the soft new snow.

He looked up at the sky and watched his breath by the starlight. The night was nice now, very cold, and as beautiful as anything a man could want. He was happy. He looked up at the stars: he had everything.

He shook it off and buttoned his Strausses and waded back to the shack.

XIV

MODERN SCIENCE TELLS US THAT LOVE IS CAUSED by the secretion in the brain of a compound known as phenylethylamine, a substance also found in chocolate. Two mysteries explained at once. Its effect on the central nervous system is virtually indistinguishable from biochemical processes associated with madness.

Chance told Elizabeth about regaling Bagley with stories from Xenophon and Virgil. Elizabeth laughed. "You'll have my ranch hands learning Latin," she said.

"Not much danger of that," he said. "Except for old Bagley. He might even take up Greek."

"Old Bean," she said. "I suppose he might."

They were sipping coffee in Elizabeth's kitchen. Skillets and long-handled pans hung from a wrought iron hoop over the stove, and windows along two walls flooded the room with winter light. Elizabeth looked out the door into her dining room for a moment, then looked back.

"Chance," she said, "I have to ask you this straight. What are your feelings for me?"

The question took him by surprise. He believed he understood his feelings, but he hadn't thought about explaining them.

"I love you, Liz. I guess my feelings are . . . I don't know. Real."

"Chance, sometimes I find myself wondering if this *is* real. Sometimes it seems too good to be true."

She looked down for a moment, then back at Chance. "I've always wondered what brings people together," she said. "Even as a little girl I pictured life as a kind of nightscape under the great cold emptiness of the sky where strangers meet by chance. Can you understand what I'm saying?" She looked into his eyes.

"I guess so."

"It's just that finding the one you are going to give yourself to is so important, but how are we to know out there under the stars? Love has always seemed a little risky to me. Frightening." She glanced down, then back at Chance. "I'm sorry, I didn't mean to do this. But I have woken at night wondering when you will decide to move on. That frightens me. I wake up sometimes with you by my side and I'm afraid. After Richard died, I swore I would never give myself to another man. But I love you, Chance. I need you. I couldn't stand to lose you too."

Chance stood, then knelt down and took her hands. "I love you," he said. "I could never leave you."

Chance understood that Elizabeth was afraid, but he did not understand the depth of her fear; he sensed it in her voice and heard it in her words, but he did not understand.

"I love you," he told her. "I'll never leave you."

Call no man happy, Sophocles wrote, till at his death he find his life a memory without pain. Chance believed he was happy—but he would not look back on this time without pain.

94

After that afternoon Elizabeth seemed pensive. When they made love she was very quiet, as if her passion had run, like the Lost River, deep underground. Chance decided to ride out to the far shack, to give her some time to be alone.

When he returned, Elizabeth was her old self again.

"Are you happy?" he said to her at dinner.

She smiled a small faint smile. "Yes," she said. "I'm sorry about the way I acted last week. I think I really am happy. But I guess I have to learn to trust happiness again. It's been a while, you know."

"Aw, tell me the truth, now. Look at everything you had here—this place, a good living, a friend like Several . . ."

"Well, you're right, of course. I do love it here, that's the only reason I stayed. Losing Richard almost undid me. I never understood that, because I had always thought of myself as a strong person—but it was a terrible time. Several was a dear friend, but I seem to need an intimacy I could never have with him. You and I have that. We share each other in ways that matter to me very much. I need to know they matter to you, too."

"Of course they do," he said, "though it's funny to think of sharing myself. I still don't know enough about myself to have anything to share."

"Oh for goodness sake, you are a great deal more than your memory."

"I'm glad you think so," he said.

They turned to business until they finished eating, but came back then to what was really on their minds.

"Tell me," she said. "What do you want for yourself?"

"Well, ma'am," he said, "I reckon it would be good for the price of beef to rise."

"Ah, but I don't reckon that answers my question, does it Mr. Chance?"

"I think I have everything else already. What else could I want?"

"Have you given up all thought of Montana, then?"

He cleared his throat and tugged at his nose and thought the question over, then cleared his throat once more. "Oh, I don't know, Liz. I don't know."

"Then what about sharing this with me? What about being part of this? You can't go on being my hired man forever."

"No," he said, "I expect not."

"I had a dream last night. I was in Philadelphia, and you had come to the city, and I was to meet you at your hotel. But I couldn't find it, and then I couldn't remember which hotel you were in, and I wandered the streets of Philadelphia trying to remember. I knew that if I didn't find it soon you would leave the city, and I would never see you again. I was so frightened that I woke. And my first thought upon waking was that now I would never find your hotel."

"I'm not staying in a hotel, Lizzy. I'm right here. I'm with you, and we have everything we need right here."

"It just seems too good to be true, Chance. Something inside me believes it's too good to be true—and so I'm afraid."

"Ah, Sweetheart," he said. "It's funny. You're unsure of the present because of the past, but I'm unsure of the past because of the present."

"Oh, Chance, I'm happy now for the first time in years. I don't think I could live if I lost you."

"You'll never lose me."

"Then make this yours, Chance. Make me yours." She looked into her cup a moment then looked up. When she spoke again her voice cracked. "Make yourself mine."

"I am yours."

"Then make an honest woman of me. What if the boys find out about us?"

96

"Well, I reckon it's a little too late to worry about that."

She stiffened and grew a little pale. "They know?"

"Of course they know."

"You *told* them?"

"I haven't told anyone a thing. Those boys may be ignorant, but they're not stupid. If you were hoping they wouldn't figure things out, you're about a month too late."

"Oh, my stars, then everyone will know. I have to deal with the other ranchers here, Chance. I can't have them thinking . . . Oh, Chance."

He knew what she wanted of him, and he thought of owning the most beautiful ranch he had ever seen, and the most beautiful woman. He believed he loved her. So he asked her to let him think a little about a future so different from that which had brought him so far.

In her bed that night he brushed her hair with his rough hand and studied her face through the darkness of her room. They wanted only to be happy together; yet Chance knew, and knew that she knew, that he would leave her soon.

XV

THE TOWN OF CRAZYWOMAN STRADDLED THE Crazywoman Creek several miles north and east of the EA ranch. According to Bean Bagley the town was not named for the creek as one might think, but for a renegade Mormon spinster who had tried to open a missionary dance hall there.

With the arrival of spring Chance needed supplies, so one balmy morning he took the buckboard to the mercantile at the edge of the town.

A man about Chance's age sat in the mercantile's wooden armchair, an Indian—a Crow perhaps, though Chance was not sure. His clothing was ordinary range attire, but he sported several strings of claws and teeth, and his boots were hand-stitched from something that must have been the skins of horned toads. His face was broad and handsome and dominated by a raptorial beak, a face born of the marriage of earth and sky. His hair hung below his shoulders, and he wore a Stetson hat so tall it could have been the lair of the north wind.

Chance placed his order and talked with the shopkeeper a while about Elizabeth and the ranch and old Several. Finally the shopkeeper told him to pull the wagon around back. As Chance turned toward the door the Indian, who had watched quietly smoking handrolled cigarettes, stopped him with a gesture.

"Don't I know you?" the man said.

"Do you?"

"I'm not sure. Are you from these parts?"

"Only recently," Chance said.

"Montana?" the Indian said, but Chance only shrugged. "You speak with a trace of Texas," the man said, "but I don't believe I know you from Texas."

"I don't reckon," Chance said.

Chance was astonished at the man's speech. He spoke perfect English, which was not unusual in itself, but his English was not that of the plains, or of the West at all—his speech was that of a Boston gentleman.

"I'm from this part of the world myself," the man said, "though not recently. I suppose I've returned to see what's become of it. I don't think I care for what I see. The Crazy Old Woman just ain't what she used to be."

His voice was sonorous and deep. It was hypnotic. Listening to his voice was like listening to the rumble of distant storms. Chance sensed as he listened that the man was a shaman, a wandering sage, perhaps, maybe from some vanished tribe. He wondered for a moment if the man spoke Latin, and must have smiled at the thought.

"That makes you laugh," the man said. "I suppose it's worth a laugh in a way. Do you know what we called this land before your people came?"

"Don't reckon I do," Chance said.

The man laughed out loud, then rubbed the back of his neck with a massive hand. "I'm sorry," he said, "I was going to make an old joke. But never mind. We called it Crazy Woman, just as you call it now. I grew up here. I'm gratified in a way that you still call the place by its name."

99

"Well," Chance said, "I call it what everybody else does. Leastwise they didn't change it."

"Might have been better if they had. But Crazywoman I suppose it will remain. Do you know how it came by that name?"

"You mean you-all had the Mormon woman too?"

The man didn't get the joke. "I don't know her," he said. "I have heard six or seven stories about the name of the place, but only one is true. I can tell it to you if you care to take the time."

A yarn. Chance decided to take the time. He sat down on a pickle barrel and folded his arms.

"When I was a child," the man said, "our village lay on this stream. It was known then by the name it bears now, though for generations before it had been called by something else. Everyone knew how it had come to be known as Crazy Woman, and sometimes on winter nights the old women of our village would tell the tale again."

"Is that so?" Chance said.

The man sat with his legs thrust in front of him, one outlandish boot crossed over the other. He held out a hand with the palm up, as if to say, "I'll tell you if you'll listen."

"Many years before I came to this world," the man said, "a young woman of our village went mad from a bitter disappointment in love. She had given birth to a daughter, but a troublesome spirit came upon her, and one day the spirit tricked her into drowning her own child.

"The young woman began that day to yip and screech like a coyote. Soon she came to be known as Crazy Woman. She became a complete stranger to everyone, possessed by a terrible spirit—a demon.

"Because of the demon, she could no longer live among our people, so the women built a lodge for her at the bend of the creek below the village. One of the women took food to her every morning while she slept.

"She lived in that lodge for many years, and all the time the spirit in her grew stronger and more fearsome. Often at night we could hear Crazy Woman howling and shouting down by the creek. The creek which had taken the spirit of her little child now kept the woman alive and fed her demon. She haunted the creek much as the spirit haunted her, so of course the creek came to be called after her."

He stubbed his cigarette on the sole of a boot, then flicked it across the room.

"As I was passing from childhood," he said, "I grew inquisitive about this crazy old woman, whom I had always heard but never seen. I decided to go down there one night to see Crazy Woman for myself.

"What I found was a horror I shall never forget, a tall old woman yipping and howling and calling out to the night sky as if to her dead child, or to the husband she had betrayed, or perhaps to some last demon, more terrible but more final than the one that raged in her now. I understood then that I should never have come. I learned then that some things are better left alone."

The man rolled a new cigarette, then lit it and passed it to Chance. He rolled and lit another for himself.

"Well," Chance said as he took a drag, "that ain't what I heard."

The Indian sprawled in his chair and laughed until Chance thought he would collapse.

"I could tell you this is the truth," the man said, "but truth is mostly what we need it to be. My truth is that Crazy Woman is dead and gone. But at least the creek and this white man's village still honor her, and that is what matters, because they honor the human condition."

"The human condition!" Chance said. It was his turn to laugh. "And what condition is that?"

"Not the best," the man said. "One of your white seers has said the world is beset with absurdities. What is the

101

story of Crazy Woman if not a story of absurdity? There are demons, you know, and they are the human condition."

I suppose I've heard that," Chance said.

"Look at the course of this thing you call civilization right here in this place," the man said. "As soon as the agents of civilization eliminated the savages, they turned against each other. The Indian wars became cattle wars. They held one right here, not long ago, white against white. Even a civilized man can see the absurdity of that."

"An adjustment," Chance said. "Now that civilization has settled in the West, we don't engage in those things any more—no more than y'all."

"Yet I hear of such a war brewing right now in the country you call Montana."

Chance's eyebrows rose. "Montana?" he said.

"That's what I'm told. I don't plan to go find out. The red man has learned his lesson: where there are white men and trouble, get scarce. Are you sure I don't know you from somewhere?"

"I don't guess I'm sure," Chance said. "But what do you know about this trouble? Do you know where it is?"

The man leaned back in his chair again, this time without laughing. "I only know what I hear, which is already more than I like. Trouble is not for me—but if trouble is what you want, I'm told you can find it in the place you call the Sally Basin. Some ranchers with an old feud about the right to own the earth."

"Who's involved?" Chance asked. "Do you know?"

The Indian shook his head and pursed his lips. "I couldn't tell you," he said.

"Do you know if it involves a Larson outfit or places called Big Sky or Paradise?"

The man laughed again. "Paradise," he said sourly. "I couldn't tell you that, either. But I can tell you this—if trouble is what you like, Sally Basin is your place."

102

XVI

A RANGE FEUD IN MONTANA. ANOTHER YARN.
Chance told himself he had put all that behind him, but he
began to wake up at night: he woke up thinking about Montana; he woke up wondering about his name; he woke up
pondering the strange note he had heard in Toejam's voice.

And when he slept, he dreamed. He dreamed of men
struggling. He dreamed of an elusive figure whose face
he could not see. And he dreamed of Crazy Woman and
her child.

In one dream he murdered the child in the creek while
the woman yipped and howled. He woke up from that
dream and dressed and went for a walk in the moonlight
along this other creek he had come to love.

He said nothing to Elizabeth, but he could tell she knew
something was on his mind.

He asked her once about the Crazywoman name.

"Oh," she said, "it seems to come from a story of a
woman who lived alone by the creek after her village was
destroyed. People stayed away from the place for years. She
was quite mad, I guess."

Elizabeth knew nothing about the renegade Mormon,
and did not know the Indian who was keeping the history

103

of the region in his small way alive. Chance did not ask her if she had heard of trouble in Montana.

Before long the stories of the Indian receded with the others into Chance's growing memory. He stopped dreaming, and Elizabeth seemed to stop waiting for him to reveal the darkest workings of his mind, and they began to inch their way toward happiness again.

But happiness, as the saying goes, too swiftly flies. Theirs took wing once more in May, and once more in a dream.

Chance was approaching a line shack on horseback in a hilly country he did not know. As he approached, he saw that the shack was in use. An old man, a Crow perhaps, or a Mexican, sat in a rocking chair in front of the open door of the shack. He smoked a pipe as he rocked himself slowly, but Chance could not make out his face. The man's clothing seemed as old as he was, and he wore an ancient Stetson so tall it could have been the lair of the north wind.

When the old man saw Chance he stopped rocking and took the pipe from his mouth and leaned back in his chair.

Chance did not like it there. The country was dry as dust; sagebrush abounded, but little cover. He could not tell whether they were alone. The corral was empty; there was not an animal in sight. There was menace in the place, a sense of peril that buzzed in the air, but Chance could not tell why.

The old man looked him over without a word. For the first time Chance had a good look at the man's face and saw then that the man was not an Indian. And he was not a Mexican.

The old man was his father.

His father said nothing as Chance approached, but watched him with unblinking eyes.

Chance wanted to talk, to find out what had become of his father, to ask him why he was in that miserable place—

yet he knew why his father was there.

The old man was the first to speak. "Is this what you'll do, then?" he asked. "You'll spend your life on someone else's place?"

"It's a good place," Chance said.

"What about your own place? You mean you'll pour your life into someone else's ranch and let your own place go to hell? Is that your destiny?"

Chance didn't know what to answer. Why wasn't he working his own ranch? He couldn't remember. He wanted to ask the old man what to do, but he could not find the words.

"What are your intentions?" his father asked.

Chance could not think of a thing.

The old man shook his head. "What hope is there for you, wasting your life like this? Even if you don't give a damn for your place in history, what about your children? Will you have their birthright be that of your woman?"

Chance still didn't answer. His father got up, shaking his head again, and went back into the shack. Chance waited for him to return but the old man did not appear. He called and waited, but the old man did not respond. He looked in the door.

The place was empty. Chance called again, then searched, inside and out, but his father was not there.

Chance rolled onto his side and looked at the woman sleeping beside him. He could not see her face as she slept, only her hair and part of a shoulder. He loved her. He was happy with her.

But the old man had been his father.

He fingered Elizabeth's hair, gently, so as not to wake her, then breathed the scent of it. He loved the smell of her hair. Yet she did not lie with him in his bed; he lay in hers. The bed, the ranch, the life—all hers. Chance loved them and knew how deeply she wanted to share them with him.

But they were not his, and marrying Elizabeth now would not make them so.

He kissed her hair and lay back on her bed, staring at the ceiling of her room, and thought for hours. And what he thought about most was his father.

The world stands on absurdities, Dostoyevsky wrote; the absurd is a necessity on earth.

Elizabeth was more important to Chance than her ranch—or his own, for that matter, if it existed at all. A little happiness was all he asked; and a little for her. But he knew at last he could not let this go. He had to know who he was, and why he had drunk himself so nearly into oblivion, and who and what he would betray if he turned his back on the past forever.

And Elizabeth knew: he could see it in her eyes. But she said nothing, and he said nothing to her.

He spent the following night alone in his cabin. The cabin, at least, was a little more his than Elizabeth's chamber in Elizabeth's palace. He lay on his back and stared at the ceiling, and wished old Several were still around. But things would have been different now, he knew, even with Several.

As he tried to recall the presence of the crusty old cowhand who had lived in that hut before him, he began to recall instead the presence of his employer on that day they had come to collect Several's things. He looked through the darkness toward the desk where she had stood fighting back her tears, and he remembered how she had looked.

He got out of bed and dressed and went out. He looked up at the palace. It hovered with its columns in the dark glimmer of the sky like the acropolis of some dusky fable.

He went up to the house and removed his boots before going in. Elizabeth was asleep in her bed. He took his clothes off and crawled in beside her.

106

She barely woke up as he put his hand on her shoulder and smelled her hair as he had done only a few hours before.

"Hello," she said.

"Hello."

She kissed him with a small kiss, then they put their arms around each other and lay still. He wanted to make love to her, yet he needed not to. As she went back to sleep, he held her in his arms as if to protect her from the absurdities and cruelties of life. Yet he knew he could not. He didn't even know if he could protect her from himself.

The question did not fade with the light of day. He didn't want to leave Elizabeth, but he knew now he had to go. He would not simply disappear into the night, as he had once before. He didn't even want to go. But he knew now that he had to.

He began to round up his gear and put in some food as he tried to think of a way to tell her.

His chance came one night at dinner as he found her watching him in her quiet way.

"What's wrong?" he said.

"I don't know. I was hoping you might tell me."

"Why do you say that?"

"Chance, I know you. You've had humors lately, and I'm not sure what they mean."

"I've had a lot on my mind," he said. "I had a visit the other night from my father."

"Your father! Why in . . ." A change darkened her face. "What are you saying?"

Chance had never seen Elizabeth more beautiful. She was wearing the white dress she had worn the night he had first joined her for dinner with Several half his life before. Yet she was more beautiful now by far than she had been that night; there was a great depth of beauty in this

107

woman, and he knew it better than anyone. Her beauty condemned him now, but he knew what he had to do.

He told her about the dream. He told her first about the Indian and his news of Montana, then told her how his father had come to him, and about recognizing his face, and about what his father had said. Then he told her he was going to Montana to settle all that for good.

"Montana!" she said.

"I'm sorry," he said. "I didn't plan this, but the whole thing has come back around, and I have to settle it."

"Oh, Chance," she said.

"I don't know how long I'll be gone," he said. "I may be back in a few days, I don't know."

"And what if you're not? What if you're gone for . . . for months? What if you find your ranch? What do you do then, stay and . . . what? Fight over it? And what if something happens to you? How will I even know?"

"Lizzy, I'll come back. I'm not leaving you, I promise."

"How can you promise me you'll come back? You won't even remember me!"

"For Christ sake, Liz."

"You don't even know what's out there, Chance. You don't know what awaits you. How can you know when you'll come back? How can you be so sure you'll even want to come back?"

"Oh for God's sake . . ."

"But you can't answer those questions, can you? Because you don't know. And what about me? If you leave me now, how can I know whether you'll ever come back?"

"Because I'm not leaving you. I'll be back in a few weeks. Whatever happens. A few weeks, Liz, then we'll know."

"'Whatever happens.' No, Chance. Do you think I'll simply lie around here like . . . like so much *liverwurst*, pining for the day you return? I can't do that, Chance. I can't wait a few weeks or a few months or however long

108

it will be just to find out whether you may return some day or not."

She got up from the table and stood for a moment. She seemed to be thinking about something. Then she turned and moved slowly into the parlor.

Chance watched her go, then put his napkin on the table and followed her. He found her in the middle of the room, chewing on her lip and gazing into the unlit fireplace.

"I have to tell you something else," she said. "I planned to tell you sooner or later anyway, so I guess this is as good a time as any." She paused for a moment. "Let's go outside," she said.

They went out onto her veranda. The evening was almost gone. The sky had taken on the darkling glow of nightfall; in the west it still held a fading light behind the somber forms of the mountains, but to the east it darkened into deepest indigo. The planet Venus was bright in the sky: the stars were coming out.

Elizabeth leaned against one of the columns and looked out across the ranch that had held her in the West. Chance stood beside another column and waited while she collected her thoughts.

"I've never told you how Richard died," she said. "To begin with, he left me. He wanted out so badly, he gave me everything—his ranch, his dream, everything. He gave them to me so there'd be nothing to keep him here. To tie him to me.

"He had to go to Connecticut on business. He told me he would be back in a month. He didn't have the courage to tell me he was leaving me, but he wrote as soon as he had left. He couldn't even wait till he got to Hartford. He wrote to me on the train and mailed his letter from Omaha. He gave me everything, Chance, so he'd never have to come back.

"I stood here many nights, just like this, hoping he would change his mind and come back." She looked at Chance a moment, then looked away. "I prayed," she said. "I ached

109

like a lovesick girl. But he never came back.

"A year later he killed himself. I guess all his dreams had fallen in. His family didn't even ask me to the funeral. They wired me after he was in the ground.

"I never understood why he left me. I couldn't understand why he did that to me. I had always thought he loved me, but he gave me everything just to get away."

She looked at Chance again, then turned away. He watched her in silence.

"So," she said. "Mr. Chance. Please don't ever speak to me of coming back. I hope you can appreciate how little I care to hear that. I'm asking you not to leave. I won't beg you, Chance, but you have to understand this—if you ride out of here, I won't expect you back." There was fear in her voice now—and resolve.

"I'm sorry," he said. "But it's not the same. I'm not leaving you, but I have to know who I am."

"I thought I knew who you are, and I loved you for it. Wasn't that enough?"

"I thought it was," he said, "but I have to do this. For God's sake, Liz, he was my father."

"Your father."

"I love you, Elizabeth, but I have to do this. However it turns out, I'll come back."

A voice that murmured from the fog in his brain told him not to be so sure, but he was not listening to that voice just then.

"I understand," she said quietly. "That mad dream is more important to you than anything. But you have to choose. If you ride out of here now, don't ever come back."

He tried to laugh, but even he wasn't convinced. "Listen to you," he said. "I've never seen you hysterical before. You'll be all right, Liz, and I'll come back, and then we'll be together forever."

She was calm now while she looked at him for a long time.

"I see I can't stop you. So go. Follow this Grail of yours. Find yourself. Be happy. But don't come back."

He almost didn't go. Elizabeth meant more to him than any goddamn ranch. He felt terrible about Richard; he hadn't even guessed. But he told himself at last that she would be all right.

He had to know who he was. The longer he put off going, the harder it would be to go. He told himself Elizabeth would be fine once he had gone. He did not understand that he was leaving her—only that he had to go.

He readied his gear, then told Bagley he was going to Montana. He asked Bagley to look after Elizabeth until his return, then loaded what he needed on the appaloosa and started north.

He rode late into the night. His nervous system was too jangled to let him stop. Well past midnight he got down and spread his roll.

He lay under the canopy of stars under which he had lain so many times before, even within memory, but he was too tired now to watch them for long—or to think.

The first color of morning touched the eastern sky as the sun prepared to rise. He hadn't thought he had ridden so long. He sat up when he realized he wasn't looking east at all, but south. The sky in the southwest was lit just like the dawn. He watched for a few seconds, then lay down and closed his eyes.

"Funny," he said to no one. "Kind of early for grassfire."

Then he was asleep.

PART TWO

The descent into hell is easy;
Night and day the gates of dark Hades
   Stand wide.
  But to turn back and trace your steps
  Once more to the open air—
    Now there's a task!

                  Virgil, *The Aeneid*
                  VI, 126-129

XVII

THE MAN WHO CALLED HIMSELF CHANCE DREW in the reins for a look around. The country was wild. The land was drier than old bones, and broken everywhere by snake-infested gullies. Here and there sandstone spines and basaltic colonnades broke the contours even more, making badlands of scrubby barrens. Chance had not seen a homestead or a rider or even a stray cow all day.

The earth rose interminably toward the west. Chance started the horse again up the faint trail they had followed since noon. The trail crossed a gully, then ascended a low ridge that rose with the land toward the afternoon sun.

He came in time to the top of that country. The west-rising ridge unfurled at the crest of a range of hills, and a new scene opened before him. Below him to the west a valley began among mountains to the south and ran northward onto the plains. Farther west, across twenty miles of grassy river bottom, rose more mountains, big ones, with snow still on their crowns.

The hills where Chance sat astride his horse tumbled down from the peaks in the south, then rose again wild and lonely to the north.

The badlands were behind him. The hills over which the trail now passed were low and dry, covered with a sparse spring grass already yellowing in the heat of the sun. The great hills to the north wore this same thin grass, but with a scattering of pines in the highest summits, miles away. In the rays of a sun that was slipping toward the mountains of the west the hills stood out, huge and silent, in hues of purple and gold.

The valley itself was mostly grass and cattle. In the distance Chance could see the glint of sunlight on a river. The place was a corner of Paradise after all, a place over which men might well fight.

The appaloosa pricked its ears and nickered just as Chance caught the drift of woodsmoke on the breeze. The trail led down the slope to a grove of aspen that suggested a spring. He started the horse toward the grove.

As he approached the camp, Chance saw that the horses wore the brand of the Big Grassy, the outfit of consequence in the Sally Basin.

He had pondered for days how best to approach the Sally Basin. Everything would depend on whether anyone recognized him. Him and his ruggedly handsome face. As long as no one did, he would have time to explore the past; but if anyone recognized that face, anyone at all, Chance knew he could find himself flung back into a past from which there might be no return.

The camp was a shack with a corral near some trees just north of the trail. Chance found three men in the camp, all armed. One stood back a little from the others, near the trees, with a Winchester in the crook of his arm. The other two stood by a cookfire before the shack, a weathered shanty with a pronghorn rack above the door.

"Howdy," he said to the men.

"How do," they said. "Get down and eat, if you'd like."

116

"Don't mind if I do. I ain't ate much since sunup. That's good country over yonder to hurry through."

One of the men at the fire was tall and heavy, with a gigantic silver concha on his belt. He was older than the other two and seemed to be in charge. The other was a skinny blond of no more than twenty.

"You drifting?" the big man said to Chance.

"Hunting work. I'm told hands are needed in the basin."

"Some are, some ain't," the man said. "You travel well heeled."

"I reckon I can cover myself if need be," Chance said, "but I prefer chasing cows."

"We could use some help chasing ours," the man said. "We had a hand run off last week—wasn't confident he could cover himself."

There was some snickering from the other men. The one with the carbine stepped toward the fire and set the rifle down, though not far from reach. "I'm Lou Calhoun," the big man said, offering his hand. "This here's Cowboy Bill," he said, nodding toward the boy beside him, "and Wyatt East."

"Chance," he said, shaking hands, "and hungrier than plain hell."

The men were eating rabbit stew. They had plenty and seemed ready to share. The coffee tasted like rodent waste.

"You know there's friction in the basin," Calhoun said.

"I've heard it."

"Not too many folks willing to ride in here looking for honest work."

"They tell me the pay's better than average here."

"Fifty and found," Calhoun said, "but you ought to be handy with that there hardware. There's been a few shots fired off around here already, so it ain't no joke about keeping yourself covered. I'm none too fond of any of that, but it's no time to pull out on them who've done for you."

"I don't much care for shooting myself," Chance said,

"but I have to admit I fancy top wages. Who do I see?"

"Sam Dancy. He's foreman on Big Grassy. We ain't heading back for two-three days yet, but tell him we sent you."

Chance sopped up brain gravy with a piece of biscuit and washed it down with a little of the coffee.

"I expect you ought to know," Wyatt East said, "we ride with a nigger hand, if that makes any difference."

Chance choked on his coffee as he rose to his feet.

"A *what*?" he said, wiping his chin. "You mean in the bunkhouse and all?"

"A Big Grassy hand don't sleep with the chickens," Calhoun said.

Chance set his coffee down and wiped his hands on his trousers and looked around at the men. He had no idea whether he had ever worked with a black cowhand, but his impulses told him he had not.

"I don't mean no disrespect," he told the men, "but I don't reckon I was raised to sleep with no coloreds."

The situation was turning awkward, but Cowboy Bill surveyed it quickly and summed it up for everyone:

"You were if you ride for Big Grassy," he said.

The Big Grassy men advised Chance to keep on traveling if he didn't want to ride with them. "There ain't no other place in this basin you'll want to work," they said. Their meaning was clear.

Chance thanked them for their food, then filled his canteen at the spring and shook the dust of the camp from his boots.

He did not know if he had made enemies there; but he had made a choice he had not been prepared to make, and had not made friends. *I'm just up from Texas, for God's sake*, he grumped to himself, and wondered again whether he had ever worked with a black hand.

The evening turned cool as it crept with purple shadows across the valley. The clean scent of spring wafted on the air, and cowbirds flitted here and there in the grass. Cattle grazed in scattered groups. Chance traveled till dusk, then bedded down near the river.

For God's sake, he mumbled as he rolled out his bed. *I come from Texas. I never figured on some colored hand.*

In the 1953 film *Shane* a mysterious rider defends a community from its enemies. In the 1973 film *High Plains Drifter* an even more mysterious rider wreaks vengeance on the community as well as its enemies. In twenty years the horse opera had become impossible; in twenty years the western hero had become a spiteful cynic; in twenty years we had discovered that a baloney sandwich really is not as good as complete happiness.

The Sally Basin's only town nestled against the foot of the mountains at the western edge of the plain. Directly behind the town a ponderosa forest rose onto a mountain that towered above the town like a darksome angel. The town was a neat and modest place for a cow town, especially for a crossroads, and betrayed little of the disquiet Chance had found on the range.

The name of the town was Larson.

The main street had two saloons. Chance picked one of the saloons and went in.

The place was dark and cool, and empty but for a rumply old man and a bar girl who sat at a corner table. A mahogany bar with a brass rail ran the length of the room, and a mirror the length of the wall. Above the whole affair presided a huge but dusty old moosehead with a protruding lip.

The bartender was a burly man with spectacles and no collar. "What's yours?" he asked.

"Coffee."

The bartender got the coffee. "Looking for someone?" he said.

119

"Work," Chance said.

"What work do you do?"

"Just cowherding."

"Have you checked with Big Grassy? They may still be short a hand."

"I run into some of their riders over east of here. They seemed a little jumpy."

"Wary of strangers," he said. "The ranchers hereabouts have never seen eye-to-eye about much, and every few years their suspicions boil up some, then there's talk of assassination and war and so on, and everybody straps on his six-shooter and sits with his back to the wall like Two-gun Dick until it blows over."

Chance was in luck. The bartender liked to talk.

"Are assassination and war in the talk now?"

"Aah," the bartender said. He took up a towel from under the bar. "There's been a little of that, but it's all talk. This has been going on so long it even has its own rules. Everybody knows the limits and when to shy up short, so that's why they're touchy about strangers."

"Meanwhile it's frightened off a feller or two of the peaceful inclination and brought the wages up," Chance said.

"That about says it."

"So if a hand don't work for Big Grassy, who does he work for?"

He ran his towel along the bar. "Rocking Tree."

"Anybody else?"

"Not in this basin. That's it."

"You mean there's only two outfits in a basin this size?"

"At one time there was only one. For a while, several years back, Grassy controlled the whole basin. That's the reason there's hard feelings now."

Chance sipped his coffee. The moose on the wall seemed amused. "So what happened?"

120

"Basin was settled by two outfits, Big Grassy and another big one called the Flying P."

Flying P, Chance thought. *Paradise*. This was too good to be true.

The barkeep tossed his towel back under the bar. "Big Grassy grazed the east side of the river," he said, "and Flying P the west, where we are now. Will Johnson of Big Grassy was said to be a tough dealer. I don't know the ins and outs of it, but old Will, I guess he held some paper on Flying P, loans or such. In the end, Flying P went bust."

A rumble of the old thunder echoed in Chance's brain. "Seems to me I heard there might have been some shenanigans in the deal."

"Who knows?" the bartender said. "Before my time. I don't reckon you can believe everything you hear."

"So for a time Johnson had the run of the basin?"

"Will and his boy Swannie. Had the run of the basin, and their brand on all the stock. They controlled enough water and grazed enough cattle in here to plain keep anyone else out—until Bert Kaffo showed up.

"I reckon Bert's pa was a wealthy feller back east. Bert come in here with a whole outfit of lawyers and the like and broke Big Grassy's hold on the lower basin, then took it over, just like that."

"And what about the Flying P? How did they get cut out so clean?"

"Don't guess anyone much knows. One story is that the old man—I can't recall his name—but he let Will and Swannie Johnson plumb steal his ranch and was too old and sick to fight back. I guess he died off, leaving the whole thing for the Johnsons."

"Didn't he have kin or anyone?"

"Don't know that, neither. There ain't hardly anyone left in the basin who was around then, except Swan Johnson, of course, and maybe a couple others. To this day Swan-

121

nie claims Bert Kaffo stole the lower basin from him with money and crooked lawyers, but others claim the Johnsons stole most of it in the first place, so there you have it. It's an old feud, and I don't reckon anything will ever change now. Been too long. Even if this thing ever really blew up, it wouldn't do much but bring in the state militia and probably get a few fellows hung. But everybody knows that. There's nothing much to it anymore but talk."

The bartender excused himself and went into the back room. He came back with a rack of whiskey glasses and began to set them out under the bar.

"Flying P," Chance said. "All sounds like the old story of the Paradise Ranch, don't it?"

"Sure," the bartender said, "that's what it is. Some folks say the Paradise was east of here, over on the Yellowstone, but this here is it, all right, if you ask me."

"Well, I'll be," Chance said. "Paradise Ranch. The romance of the West ain't dead after all, eh?"

The bartender laughed. "Not at all. Now if I could only figure a way to get romance to sell whiskey—"

"I expect a hand could do worse than to ride for a legend and make top pay doing it. You know if Rocking Tree is hiring?"

"Oh, with the calf hunt coming on, I wouldn't be surprised."

The bartender described the geography of Sally Basin while Chance drank coffee and the moose looked on.

The Big Grassy Ranch lay at the foot of the Big Grassy Mountains up the basin to the south, on the other side of the river. Rocking Tree occupied a site several miles the other direction, due north of the town. Each outfit grazed its cattle on its end of the basin, with the town about in the middle.

"Rocking Tree took up the old Flying P homestead, or what?"

"No, no, Flying P was just across the river from Big Grassy, up where the Sally comes out of the mountains. Ain't there no more, though."

"I'm told there's been some shooting," Chance said.

"More coffee?" the bartender said. Chance nodded, and the barkeep refilled his cup.

"Swannie says he's been losing some stock," the bartender said, "and claims it's part of a plan of Bert's to squeeze him off the range. There's been talk of both outfits throwing pretty wide loops, but there's been more words on the subject than there ever were calves in this basin. Some Grassy hands claim they jumped a crew trying to drive a gather of their young stuff onto Rocking Tree grass one night and run them off with a few shots. Rocking Tree says it's all malarkey and has been sending out night riders to keep its own herd from catching the wanderlust, as they say."

"So who's right?"

The Bartender removed his spectacles and wiped them on his shirt. "Mister," he said, "I sell whiskey for the gentleman that owns this place. And coffee. I figure right is whoever has cash money and don't get caught with his pants around his ankles." He put his spectacles back on.

"Fair enough," Chance said, "but let me ask you one more thing."

"Ask away."

"How did the town come to be called Larson? Could that have been the name of the feller at the Flying P?"

The bartender laughed again. "No," he said, "no no. Larson's Mercantile. First store in the basin. Town grew up around it."

"And who was Larson?"

"Swede, pioneered in from Dakota or somewheres with a wagon of goods. Daughter runs the place now. Fine folks."

"Well, in any case I need a job. You say Rocking Tree is north of here?"

"Ten or twelve miles. You might check in first with the constable. We do have law here, and he likes to know who's in town."

Chance settled up for the coffee and thanked the bartender and went out into the street.

The sheriff was a fat, balding man with a neat mustache. He had tiny eyes and sweat on his brow, but he watched from those eyes with something that made Chance take note. He was sitting with his feet on his desk, cleaning his fingernails. He got to his feet with noticeable effort.

"What can I do for you?" the Sheriff said. His voice rasped like a crosscut saw.

"I'm looking for work," Chance said. "Barkeep said you like to screen the applicants."

"Hm," he rumbled. "Who are you applying with?"

"Whoever needs hands."

"Big Grassy's still looking for a hand."

"I'm told Rocking Tree is closer to town."

"So it is. You like to come to town, do you?"

"Ever know a cowpoke who didn't?"

"I see you left your hardware put away. We like it that way here."

"I don't expect an honest man wears his iron in town without cause."

"I don't expect so either—and I don't expect an honest man finds cause."

"There is some talk of feuding around here."

The Sheriff reached into his shirt pocket and took out a match stick, which he stuck like a cigarette between his lips. He sat down and looked up at Chance.

"If that's what brought you to Sally Basin," the sheriff said, "you best climb back on that palousy and move along. There hasn't been no trouble here, and there ain't going to be."

"I'm not looking for trouble, Sheriff, but I'm not afraid of

124

it and I'm told there's top pay in the bargain."

"We'll see," the sheriff said. "The ranchers here don't much care for each other. That's the long and short of it. And I don't much care for either of them. That's why folks elected me, they know I won't take sides. My job is the law, and anybody crosses it deals with me. The town backs me up on that."

"Do you mind my asking what the rumpus is about, then?"

The Sheriff folded his arms across his belly. "Bert and Swannie like to think the Basin isn't big enough for both of them, but that's all sheepshit, and they both know it, so we have a kind of homeostasis here, as they like to say."

"Homeostasis," Chance said.

He didn't ask about the Flying P. He didn't think the sheriff shared his enthusiasm for the past.

"As for the stories of night riders," the sheriff said, "I trust I don't need to explain how this state deals with rustlers or murderers."

"Sheriff, I believe the best diplomacy is straight talk, and you certainly have given me that."

The Sheriff rose to his feet once more. "Go on down to Rocking Tree, then, if you've a mind to. If Bert ain't hiring, I reckon Swannie is."

Chance unhitched the appaloosa and started north along the Rocking Tree road. The sun had slipped behind the mountains when he caught sight of the buildings of Rocking Tree Ranch.

XVIII

ROCKING TREE RANCH FED ITS CATTLE ON ACREAGE half the size of Rhode Island. The two ranches of the Sally Basin shared enough land to form their own state—if they could just agree to do it. But they couldn't.

They did agree on one thing. Barbed wire had never been strung between them. Both Swannie Johnson and Bert Kaffo were said to have claimed they would see the insides of their graves before they would see fence wire hung in the Sally Basin. But their stubbornness allowed their herds to mingle, especially when thunderstorms sent cattle fleeing for their lives.

The hands themselves harbored little of the hostility of their employers. They were just cowboys. But as the bartender had said, even the cowboys had grown edgy.

Bert Kaffo remained aloof in his tall Victorian house and never mixed with the men. Chance saw him rarely, and only from a distance.

His foreman was an imposing man named Fil Hazzard, a large man with a rectangular face and a natural squint in his eye.

Fil Hazzard ran the operations of the ranch. Everyone understood that decisions on the Rocking Tree came from the tall house, but they came through Fil. The men of the Rocking Tree were paid by Bert Kaffo—but they worked for Fil Hazzard.

Fil was a demanding boss, Chance thought, but a good one. He treated the men with respect, but like Mr. Kaffo himself, he remained somewhat aloof.

Spring branding had been delayed by rain and was just getting under way. Fil assigned Chance with several other hands to work the upper basin on the other side of the river.

Their job was simple: to search Big Grassy range for Rocking Tree cattle. Any unbranded calves with Rocking Tree mothers would be herded onto Rocking Tree grass and branded, then the men would start the process over on their own range. Big Grassy hands would follow the same routine working from the Rocking Tree end of the basin.

Chance and his bunch rode straight for the Big Grassy. They crossed the river, then split into smaller groups to fan out across the plain. Chance and two other hands rode south along the river toward the ranch while the others rode east toward the hills.

One of Chance's companions was a gangly man called Chappadquiddick, a funny-looking man with a long jaw and thinning hair and a forehead high enough to make its own weather. The other, known as Nyes, was about thirty and handsome as a movie star. He had green eyes and a flaming red beard, though his hair was not red at all.

The men rode south to within a mile of the Big Grassy corral. They camped by the river at a spot where a meander had created almost an island.

The spot made a nice place for a camp. To the south and west they were surrounded by mountains. To the east and northeast rose the hills. And to the north lay nothing but

127

grass, as far as they could see.

They built a cowchip fire. Chappaquiddick began baking biscuits in an oven he had cut from a two-gallon tin and carried with him wherever he went.

While the biscuits rose and the gravy simmered and the men sat drinking coffee, three riders approached from the north. Chappaquiddick got up and walked to his horse. He slipped his Winchester from its boot.

"Trouble?" Chance said.

"Naw," Nyes said, "but we're on range used by other folks. No harm in caution."

The riders came without hurry toward the camp. They were Big Grassy men. They rode into camp but remained mounted.

"Evening," one of the riders said. "Bit far from home, ain't you?"

"A sight farther than you-all, I reckon," said Nyes.

The rider who spoke was a young man with an easy, cocky manner. "I guess I know you good enough," he said to Chappaquiddick and Nyes, "but who are you?" The question did not strike Chance as a challenge, but neither was it simple cowhand charm.

"Chance," he said. "Climb down and have some of this fine coffee."

The young man did not get down. Nyes shrugged. "No offense," he said. "Tastes like gopher grunt anyway."

"You boys are kind of far off your range," the young man said again.

"Well it's the calf hunt, Elroy. We didn't figure you'd gather our stock and bring it to us."

"Listen, Nyes, we're missing young stuff. There's no Rocking Tree stock up this far on this side of the river, and I reckon we'll appreciate it if you don't come sniffing around our herd."

128

"Don't get your tail in such a knot, Elroy," Nyes said, "we're just starting our sweep. You think we'd camp in your front yard before a midnight ride?"

"Just see that you stay put till morning. We're riding nightwatch and we don't want to see anyone easing out of here by starlight."

"Rocking Tree don't ride by no starlight, Elroy. Stay here with us, if you're not afraid for your scalps."

"You just mind what I'm telling you. And you tell Bert we've seen the last of our losses."

"I'll tell him, Elroy," Nyes said.

The Big Grassy riders turned away and the Rocking Tree men went back to their cooking and their coffee.

"Well," Chance said when the riders were gone, "who was *that*?"

"Elroy," said Nyes.

Chappaquiddick nodded as he squatted down to tend his biscuits. "It was Elroy," he said.

"Since I ain't been party to your range disputes here, maybe you-all can tell me what I've rode into."

"The way some folks see it," Nyes said, "the main problem in this basin is us. Used to be a time when Big Grassy grazed this whole basin. I expect squatters tried to move in over the years, but the Johnsons discouraged that sort of thing, till Bert come in and took up an old claim and stayed. Swannie says the shock of it killed his pa, and he ain't ever forgiven Bert."

"What's the rub with old Elroy, then? He seemed to take us kind of personal."

"Swannie's boy. Heir to the basin, he'd like to think."

"What about the missing stock?"

"Mostly talk, far as I can tell. Nobody's really had a chance to count head yet. I think it's mostly Elroy's fluids eating at him, but I reckon we'll know soon enough."

"Tell me about the shooting."

129

"More Big Grassy talk, I reckon," Chappaquiddick said. "They're talking about shooting at us, but as far as I know, we ain't been shot at yet, so I don't know who it might've been."

"Bohemian pirates, maybe?"

"Well, I expect we'll know more when we see whether the herds have actually shrunk of late."

Chance split some of Chappaquiddick's biscuits and smothered them with chipped beef and gravy. He poured a fresh cup of coffee and looked up along the hills.

"What about the outfit that was in here before Will Johnson?" he said.

"Wasn't much of an outfit," Nyes said. "I don't know whether he lost his herd or what, but by the time Bert showed up there wasn't nothing left but a couple of buildings."

"Now, where in the purple hell did you hear that?" Chappaquiddick said, wiping gravy from his mouth. "First outfit in this basin was bigger than Big Grassy is today. Flying F, it was called."

"Bull whacky," Nyes said, and the men commenced a campfire disputation that told Chance neither of them knew enough to be any help.

"Don't look like you'll find much agreement here," Nyes said.

"I imagine Swannie could tell you the whole of it," Chappaquiddick said, "but I wouldn't go around asking him. I've heard he's a little touchy on the subject of the past."

"I'll tell you who might, though," said Nyes. "Maggie. She could tell you for sure." He looked at Chappaquiddick. "Now ain't that right?"

Chappaquiddick nodded. "Maggie," he said.

"That's right," Nyes said. "Over at the mercantile. Probably knows the history of the place as good as dang near anybody."

130

Chappaquiddick nodded again. "Except for Swannie," he said.

Chance got up and walked over to the riverbank. The water was clean and swift as it swept around that point of sod, and scraps of bark from upstream woods danced on the sandy bottom like figures waltzing. He watched them for several minutes and listened to the quiet music of the water and wondered about the past from which there might be no return.

Big Grassy owned the parks and bottoms behind the ranch outright, so the Rocking Tree hands did not venture into the head of the basin. For the next three days they worked downstream, checking brands and herding Rocking Tree stock.

"Seems like Elroy may be right," Chappaquiddick said in camp. "I'm seeing more childless she-critters up here than ticks on a sheepdog."

"Does seem a little queer," Nyes agreed. "Swannie has a fair calf herd here, but too many uncalved cows."

When they met with the men who had swept the eastern flank of the basin they heard the same story. Too many cows simply had no calves.

They were met near the river by fresh hands from the Rocking Tree, and the group split up again. Chance set out northward along the foot of the eastern hills to beat the thickets and draws for cows.

Several miles north of the cabin where Chance had met Calhoun and the others, a grassy arm descended out of the hills and into the basin. A handful of cows had wandered up the arm following the graze. Chance drove them down onto open range, then crossed over the lower reach of the arm toward a draw on the other side.

Halfway down to the draw the appaloosa pulled up stiff-legged and froze. A low and ghastly sound rose from a

131

thicket just below them, a moaning and gasping that, whatever it was, could only mean trouble.

The appaloosa would go no further. Chance tethered it to a bush and started down toward the thicket with his Winchester in hand.

In the trees he found a horse, a saddled Big Grassy roan, lying in its own blood by the edge of the stream. Its eyes were like small moons as it struggled against some unseen tormentor and gasped for breath.

The roan appeared to have been there a day or so. Chance could not tell how it had been hurt; it seemed to be lying on its wound. He wanted to put it away, but decided not to risk a shot until he knew what had happened. And what had become of the rider.

He left the thicket and backtracked the roan upstream into the draw. Soon the tracks were met by others, three sets, all leading into the draw. One set was those of the roan itself; the other tracks looked a little older. Only those of the roan returned.

The draw angled to the right and opened into a broad gully that opened in turn into a box canyon a little beyond. Chance moved carefully to the mouth of the canyon, then crouched by a boulder, where he watched and listened for signs of life. At the far end of the canyon stood another thicket, and along the right flank yet another.

Something between the stream and the thicket to the right caught Chance's eye. A man, a body, perhaps, lay in the grass. Keeping one eye on the thickets and one on the hills, Chance came out into the open.

The man, wearing cowhand clothes, was black. Chance was a little surprised, but remembered well enough the black hand at Big Grassy. The man had been gored in the leg, and like the horse had lost blood. He was alive but only partly conscious. He was hot with fever, but shivered as he lay in the sun.

Chance gave him a drink from his hat, then cut the leg of his jeans away. The wound was nasty; it looked like an evil grin. Chance washed it out as well as he could, then left to get his horse.

He destroyed the roan in the thicket, then removed the saddle and set it in the crotch of a tree away from the creek. He picked up the bedroll and found his own horse and led it over the arm well above the roan.

He returned to the thicket by the injured man and laid out the man's bedroll. He carried the man from the creek and put him into the bed, then built a fire and began to gather wood.

As he was dragging a length of alder to the fire, a new sound echoed in the canyon, an ominous sound Chance recognized at once. A slate-dark crossbreed bull had emerged from the far thicket and was watching him with bull-righteous paranoia.

Chance gave the man more water and bathed his face and fed him a little coffee, all the while wary of the bull. The man needed the doctor but was not fit to be moved, and the bull was on the prowl. Chance cursed. He had work to do, and here he was nursemaiding the same goddamned colored he hadn't wanted to work with in the first place.

He cursed again and added wood to the fire and ate some jerky, then sat down against a tree with his carbine on his lap and managed to fall asleep.

XIX

AS NIGHT FELL, THE INJURED MAN BEGAN TO SHIVER. Chance was afraid his shaking would beat him to death, so he gave the man his blankets and built a second fire to keep him warm on both sides. He wrapped himself in his slicker and sat against the tree again and tried to sleep. He was pursued all night by visions of the crossbreed bull, and twice in the dark he was awakened by snorts from the canyon.

In the morning the man was no better. He was growing delirious and his wound was festering. There seemed to be no sign of blood poisoning, but Chance didn't know what to look for in the dark skin. He cursed again.

The bull was quiet in his keep. Chance rode up onto the arm and down to where he could get a look into the basin, hoping to spot someone who could go for help. No one was in sight.

That night the man moaned and struggled and babbled in some wild fantastic tongue. The bull snorted. Chance drifted in and out of troubled sleep.

The next morning the man was awake, and had stopped shaking. He raised his head and tried a grin that quickly turned to grimace.

"I don't feel so good," he said.

"You ought to see the way you look," Chance said.

"I expect that critter done hurt my horse worse than it hurt me."

"If he hears you're awake, he may hurt you worse yet."

The man sat up but promptly lay back down. "Maybe that ain't such a bad idea," he said.

The man appeared to be a few years older than Chance. His hair was mostly gray, and he had the sinewy build of someone who had made his living by hard work. Healthy, the man might be one to be reckoned with, but he was hardly healthy now.

"I figure you'll need a doc before you're on your feet again," Chance said. "You sure ain't fit to ride now. Do you think you can keep that bull out of your jeans if I hightail it for town?"

"I don't think there's much in my jeans he want," the man said, "long as I don't try to chase him from them trees."

Chance rode down to the lower draw and retrieved the man's saddle. The carbine was missing from its boot. He brought the saddle back to the camp and set it where the man could prop himself up on it, then laid his Winchester beside the saddle.

"You keep an eye on that mountain of hellfury up there," he said, "but be careful who you use this thing on. I'd hate to have you shoot the basin's only doc."

"If I have any more of them dreams," the man said, "I may be out of ammunition before the doc even come."

"Who can I tell him he's coming for?" Chance said.

"Just tell them Black Moses sent you. And leave word in town for Sam Dancy. I don't want him giving away my bunk while I'm still on duty."

135

Chance rode down off the arm and struck for the Rocking Tree, which was closer than the town.

Rocking Tree hands knew Black Moses, and four or five said they knew the canyon. Fil Hazzard sent two men with a buckboard back to the canyon while Chance started for town with a fresh horse.

In town Chance found the doctor and left word for Big Grassy that Black Moses was hurt. When he returned to the draw with the doctor, the Rocking Tree men had made fresh coffee.

The doctor treated the wound, then they carried the injured man on a litter to the wagon.

The beast in the trees snorted and stamped and came out into the open. The hand called Cutbank kept watch with a big Sharps, a buffalo gun they had brought for that purpose.

With evening coming on and Black Moses in the wagon, the doctor started for town. Chance and the others stayed to finish working the draws.

They used the Sharps, which sounded like the battleship *Maine* in that canyon, to drive the bull back onto open range. A bull in the herd, they said, was worth two in the bush. They drove him away from the hills, then camped by the creek to discourage his return.

As the life of the Sally Basin began to flow from the rhythms of spring to the sultry measures of summer, one thing was now clear: the entire calf herd of the Sally Basin was smaller than it should have been.

Chance was impatient to learn more about the basin and its past. When roundup was finished he waited for a free Saturday afternoon, then put on his only clean shirt and made his way to town.

He rode straight to Larson's store. The place was stocked with everything a frontier mercantile could hold, tables of clothing, bins of foodstuffs, and shelves of housewares and knicknacks and vegetables in cans. A girl of thirteen or fourteen was minding the place.

"Howdy," he said.

"Good afternoon." She was a pretty child with blue eyes and straw hair in pigtails.

"My name's Chance. I'm new at the Rocking Tree. You must be the Dark girl."

"Yes sir," she said. "Pleased to meet you."

Chance brought tobacco and shaving soap to the counter, then looked at some new shirts and asked a few questions.

"My ma knows more about the old days than I do," the girl said. "Maybe you can ask her sometime. Just now she's busy with the cooking."

Chance put two new shirts beside the soap and tobacco on the counter. He wanted to talk with the woman, but he saw how things were.

"I reckon that would be nice," he said. "Maybe I can do that next time I'm in. Tell your ma I was by."

He paid for his merchandise and left the store. He left the shirts and soap in his saddlebags and had supper at the Moosehead, which was livelier than it had been the day he arrived.

As Chance finished his steak and potatoes, Chappaquiddick and a hand named Simon Wheeler arrived with several others from the Rocking Tree. They joined him and ordered a bottle. He watched the men pour the lovely liquid into little glasses, and remembered the good feel of whiskey in the mouth.

"Drink?" someone said to Chance.

Chance frowned. "Boys," he said, "y'all couldn't drink with me."

The boys erupted in a round of cowhand hilarity. One of them poured Chance a drink, but Chance slid it back with

137

a wink. "What I want to know," he said, "is what a body does for companionship in these parts."

"Haw, haw," the boys said, slapping their legs and downing their whiskeys. Two or three rose to their feet. "Well, come on," they said.

The basin's only funhouse was a raggedy operation composed of a row of tents along an alley behind the town. The girls were unattractive and expensive, but Chance had not been with a woman since leaving Wyoming. He went into a tent with a woman known as Vanity. She was a homely thing with oily skin and matted hair, but she knew her trade. Chance was not tempted to spend the night.

When he was done, he returned to the Moosehead with Chappaquiddick for coffee, then left for the ranch. The ride was long for that time of night, but it gave him a chance to think.

Poking Vanity had been fun, but Vanity was not Elizabeth. He hadn't let himself think much about Elizabeth since leaving her ranch. He let himself think a little about her now.

He missed her. He hoped she was okay. A feeling that crept along his back told him he would rather be with her now than pursuing this madness, but he shrugged that feeling off.

He thought about a story he had read. A boy was being sent into the camp of the enemy to do the work of a spy. He was trained for the work by a man who knew things the boy had never guessed. One day the man threw a jug onto the floor, where it shattered. Then as the boy watched, the fragments began to move across the floor, drawn slowly together by the force of his teacher's voice.

Fragments of Chance's mystery lay all around him. He sensed that a handful of pieces were still missing, but he hoped Maggie Dark could provide those pieces—and that the power of her voice would start them coming together.

He had a good moon; the world was all shadows and shifting light. To Chance's left, beyond the fringe of trees, the mountains rose to the sky. Across the way the sleeping hills seemed suspended in the night. Somewhere in the basin coyotes yipped and called.

He thought once more about Elizabeth, and was thinking of her when he reached the Rocking Tree.

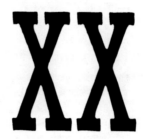

XX

THE MESS ROOM OF THE ROCKING TREE FED THIRTY hands. The cook was known as the Executioner, but no one refused to eat.

One evening Fil Hazzard announced that Chance was wanted for supper that Saturday at the Big Grassy. Swannie wanted to thank him for saving the life of one of his hands.

Chance didn't see how he could decline. He wasn't ready for this, but no matter: he would meet Swan Johnson as his guest.

When Saturday came, he finished his morning's work and wrapped a new shirt in his bedroll, then saddled the appaloosa and started off.

Chance rode in from the north and met the road from Larson just before it entered the Big Grassy gate. He thought once more about his face. It felt like a beacon, a flaming lamp out of the past. One thing held in his favor: his face had been kicked in a time or two since last he might have met Swannie Johnson.

The headquarters of the Big Grassy were bigger than any Chance could remember. The house was a large two-story

140

building of mountain granite with a split shake roof. It stood on a low rise overlooking the basin. The buildings and corrals lay behind, between the house and a stand of pines that marked the place the Big Grassy Mountains rose out of the earth.

The road led up behind the house to a pole corral and a cluster of sheds. At the corral a wiry gray-haired man walked out to meet him.

"You're Chance?" he asked.

"That's what my mother called me."

"Sam Dancy," the man said. "Climb down and I'll show you the bunkhouse. Then you can care for your horse. Supper ain't for a bit yet, so you can clean up at the bunkhouse if you like."

There was nothing in Dancy's face that said he had ever seen Chance before. Dancy led Chance to the bunkhouse. Several hands were there, including Wyatt East, whom he had met on the range, and Black Moses.

Chance took care of the appaloosa, then washed up at the bunkhouse and put on his clean clothes. Black Moses was doing the same.

"You still look a little pale," Chance said.

"Not as pale as I feared I might by now."

"How's the leg?"

"Not too good. At least they didn't have to take it."

Chance answered with a nod, then slicked back his hair and went outside. Dancy came up from the house. With Moses on crutches, the three men walked to the house and went in.

In the parlor a darkly handsome man rose when they entered. The man was about Chance's age and about Chance's height, clean-shaven and lean but muscular. He looked as though he was accustomed both to hard work and comfort. He seemed comfortable here in his home.

"Swannie," Dancy said, "Rocking Tree's Chance. Chance, Swanson Johnson, owner of this outfit."

Swanson Johnson offered his hand. He was about to speak, then seemed to hesitate as he studied Chance's face. He only paused for a moment, but that moment seemed to Chance to cover the span of twenty years.

"My pleasure," Swannie said.

Swannie smiled as he shook Chance's hand, but Chance was certain he traced a flicker of confusion in his eyes.

"Drinks, gentlemen?" Dancy asked as they sat down.

"Coffee for me," Chance said.

Elroy entered the room and sat down in an armchair not far from his father. "I'll take one of them," he said, tossing a glance at the whiskey in Swannie's hand. Dancy left the room.

"Chance," Swannie said, "I believe you've met my boy Elroy."

Chance and Elroy nodded. "Evening," they said.

"Moses tells me you saved his life."

"Had to," Chance said. "I was low on coffee."

"Good thing you happened into that draw when you did," Swannie said. From under dark brows he seemed to be watching Chance.

"Reckon so," Chance said. "Your man was indisposed at the time, and that behemoth was still deliberating its options."

"I'm sure it was," Swannie said. "Whose brand was it wearing, do you know?"

"Rocking Tree. Me and Simon Wheeler drove it out of there later."

"Well," Swannie said again, "just a good thing you came along when you did." He seemed to be making a point.

Chance recalled the tracks he had found leading into Moses' canyon. He had almost forgotten: the tracks had led into the canyon but not back again. He didn't mention that now.

142

When the drinks were gone, Swannie led the men into his dining room. They were joined there by Swannie's wife, a plump woman with frizzy hair who seemed at ease but said little. Chance found himself seated beside Black Moses.

He didn't say much to Moses; it was not that he actually disliked the man, he simply didn't know how to deal with him.

Twice Chance looked up to discover Swan Johnson watching him in silence. No one else seemed to notice. Except for his interest in Chance's account of finding Moses and keeping watch for the bull, Sam Dancy showed Chance no more interest than he would have shown anyone else.

But Swannie watched.

Near the end of the meal, Swannie looked up from his plate again.

"Where did you say you're from?" he asked.

"Don't guess I said. Texas, mostly, lately out of Wyoming." Chance could speak the drawl like a native, and had spoken that way all evening.

"Texas," Swannie said, as if to let it sink in. "Have you ever worked in Montana before?"

"Not before I hired on with Bert about a month ago. Ever been to Texas?"

"No," Swannie said, almost to himself. He seemed to look for a moment at something in the middle of his long table, then looked up at Chance again.

"What brings you to Montana?" he said.

Something was working on Swannie's mind. Chance did not know whether Swannie was given to fits of contemplation, but Swannie seemed to have grown strangely thoughtful about Texas. Chance decided to give this a nudge to see where it would lead.

"Oh," he said, rocking back on his chair as if to weave a history of his travels, "I was getting fidgety down there in Texas and decided to wander up along the country a little.

143

Feller I met told me of a place in Montana he thought I'd like. Paradise Ranch, he called it. Ever hear of it?"

This time there was no mistaking the look on Swannie's face. He stared at Chance for a moment.

"Yes," he said. "I suppose everybody in these parts has heard of it."

"Fellers at Rocking Tree tell me it's over east somewhere, maybe over by Miles City or so."

"No," Swannie said. "Paradise Ranch was a story started by an eastern newspaper writer wanting to resurrect the glory of the West. That was ten or fifteen years ago, wasn't it, Sam?"

Dancy nodded. His face said nothing.

"There's no Paradise Ranch," Swannie said. "Never was. I guess that story must still be making the rounds—at least in Texas."

Swannie seemed to be wrestling with this. He did not like it. And he did not seem to know what to think about Chance.

After the table had been cleared, Swannie's wife made pleasantries with her guests, then disappeared as the men retired once more to the parlor.

Swannie passed out cigars and settled into his leather chair. He lit his cigar and took a long pull, then slowly exhaled a stream of the smoke toward the massive beams of his fortress.

"Chance," he said, "I asked you to my home because you saved the life of one of my men, and for that I'm grateful. I expect you know that things aren't well between your employer and myself. Never have been. But things may be taking a turn for the worse, and I suppose I owe you the courtesy of letting you know. Big Grassy is missing a substantial number of young stock. That has happened before, and I have reason to believe that Bert is behind it."

"All I know is that Rocking Tree is having the same problem. If I may speak freely, the feeling there is that

144

Grassy is behind it. What I don't understand is why no one wants to consider the obvious—that someone else is stealing from both of y'all."

"Chance, I don't make judgments based on feelings, and I don't make idle accusations. I have reason to believe that Bert Kaffo is behind the stealing in this basin, and I can tell you it is going to stop. I'm afraid that may mean trouble, but my trouble is with Bert. Most of his hands are good men. My complaint is not with them. And unless you are involved in this thing, my complaint is not with you, either. You've done me a service, and I feel I owe you at least the consideration of letting you know where things stand. This is not a threat or a warning, but if you don't want to be mixed up in trouble not of your own making, I suggest you leave Sally Basin and take as many good men with you as you can, before people get hurt."

"But what would Bert stand to gain from either a rustling operation or a showdown?"

"I don't want to go into the history of it, but I can tell you this—I don't make idle accusations, and the stealing is going to stop. It's that simple. Anyone who is not part of it would be well advised to haul out."

Chance thanked him for his advice, but wondered if it hid a threat just the same.

"Well," Swannie said, "bed time. Chance, you are welcome to spend the night here in the bunkhouse."

"Thanks, but I have to start back tonight. I expect I'll want to be in church in the morning. Hope to see some of y'all there."

The suggestion drew a laugh from Elroy, but Swanson Johnson said nothing. Chance thanked the Johnsons again, then saddled his horse and turned down the road toward the town called Larson.

145

XXI

THE ONLY CHURCH IN LARSON STOOD AT THE north end of the main street, a chalky deacon presiding over the whole length of the town.

Chance had spotted the Dark girl before the service. She was with a woman who appeared to be her mother. When the service was over he approached them while they talked with friends.

"Morning, Miss," he said to the girl.

The girl introduced him to her mother, a slender woman with flaxen hair who made Chance think of summer.

"You're the man who saved Big Grassy's Moses," said Maggie Dark.

"I expect so, ma'm, if you can call building a campfire saving a man."

"I imagine Moses has gotten less from some men," she said. "Sissy tells me you have an interest in the history of our town."

"I believe I may have had kin in these parts at one time. They may still be here, for all I know."

"If they are," she said, "I'm sure I know them. Do you know their name?"

"I don't reckon I do, unless it's the same as ours."

146

"Chance?" No, not anywhere in this part of Montana that I can think of. Did they have their own place? Cattle ranch?"

"I expect so, but I'm not sure where. I left Texas a couple years ago to see the rest of the world, and when I found myself in Montana, I told myself I ought to see if I could locate any such folks I might have. Sally Basin, I seem to recall. Folks tell me you know the history of this area about as good as anyone."

"Well, I suppose so, except maybe for Mr. Johnson and one or two of his men. Why don't you join us for dinner? Maybe you'll remember something I'll recognize."

Chance pretended feebly that he had somewhere else to go, but she insisted, so he pretended to give in.

They walked to Maggie's home at the store. The family quarters were over the shop, but the kitchen and the dining room were behind it, pleasant rooms with pine wainscoting and blue-checkered curtains. Large windows flooded the place with light and gave it an airy feeling Chance liked.

Maggie had stewed a chicken. Her family was all there— the girl, a son two or three years younger, and her hired hand, a seventeen- or eighteen-year-old named Walter Hawkins. Walter did not live with Maggie and her children, but in the town's only hotel, a place known, for reasons Chance could only surmise, as the Slaughter House.

The food and the company in Maggie's home were both better than those in the messroom of the Rocking Tree. As usual, he answered the questions about himself without really answering at all.

"And what about you?" he said to Maggie. "You were born in these parts?"

"Yes," she said, "right upstairs. My father built this store, and started the town, really. It's named for him, you know."

"Yes," he said, "I expect I heard that. Larson. Fella in

147

Texas once mistook me for a Montana Larson, but I don't believe I know of any Larson kin of mine."

"There are certainly plenty of us in Montana, mostly immigrants from the old country. Minnesota, you know."

Chance laughed. "I don't reckon Dark is a name you hear much, though," he said.

"Why, thank you," she said. "I have been wanting to ask you about your own name, Mr. Chance, but I didn't want to seem forward."

Chance laughed again. "California name," he said. "Very old. First Chance in America came with Sir Francis Drake and stayed. Family migrated east into Texas while everyone else was moving west. Always been a little unpredictable, I expect."

Now Maggie and the children laughed. "Well, I believe I can match that," she said. "You see, the Dark family was not named for the chaos of night, as one might think, though I half suspect it yet."

"I give up, then," Chance said.

"It's a French name, you see. My husband's people were Canadian. Tom swore he was a direct descendent of Joan of Arc—Sainte Jeanne d'Arc, the patron saint of France."

"Well I'll be," Chance said. "Then that makes these here younkers descendants of the saint as well, though you yourself are none."

"As they often remind me," she said. "But of course we are not Catholic, so they have to mind me anyway."

"And you grew up here?" he asked.

"Right here," she said.

"I've heard tell of a place called the Paradise Ranch, said to have been in these parts. Ever hear of it?"

Maggie laughed again. "Oh my, yes," she said. "I think that story was old when I was a child. I personally believe it was brought into these parts from Texas when this country was first opened up to ranching."

148

"So you don't believe there ever was such a place?"

"Not around here. I've heard quite a few versions of that story. I imagine they include things that happened in the old days. I guess the early days of Texas were quite something. Anything could have happened in those days. But nothing like that ever happened here."

"Wasn't there an outfit in here once called the Flying F, or one of them other alphabet outfits?"

She laughed. "Flying P, yes, the first ranch in the basin."

"One of the fellas told me he thought that's where the Paradise Ranch story came from."

"Oh, yes, I've heard that. I suppose Flying P fits the story a little, but I believe the Paradise Ranch legend is older than any of the ranches we ever had in the Sally Basin."

"I see," Chance said. "Hard to know what to believe sometimes, ain't it?"

When everyone was finished, the children cleared the table, and Maggie served up rhubarb pie with coffee. The coffee was weak by cowhand standards, but at least it tasted like actual coffee.

Chance liked Maggie Dark. She was rather pretty with her yellow hair and clear blue eyes. Her upper lip was funny; it came a little too high, as if she had failed to stay inside the lines with pale rouge. But it was pretty in its way, and she was pretty. She was a good person, too, he could tell.

"Tell me about the basin," Chance said. "Who settled it? Who actually has ranched here?"

"Well, my papa settled here in '70, probably the worst fool thing anybody ever did, with the uprisings and all. He loved this spot. 'Prettiest townsite in the West,' he called it. He knew cattlemen would move in soon, and he picked this spot because the traffic on this trail assured him a trade even without them.

"But the cattlemen were not long in coming. A man

149

from Texas brought in a large herd and began grazing it on just about the whole basin. Two or three years later he brought in a partner. Both men were retired officers, I believe, and had some money. They managed to acquire all of the important water rights in the basin, but once they had control, they split up."

"And that's how Big Grassy got its start."

"That's right. Swannie's father, Will Johnson."

"And Flying P?"

"Millard Quackenbush," she said.

"Quackenbush!" he said. For the second time since his arrival in the Sally Basin he was obliged to wipe his coffee from his chin. "Quackenbush?"

"Why, yes," Maggie said. "You know the name?"

Chance poked at his shirtfront with his napkin and wondered for a moment if he had ever been known as Ebenezer Quackenbush. "No," he said, "not that I recall. Funny name, though. Wonder why they didn't call it the Flying Q."

"I think Millard named it for his wife. I don't remember her name—I never knew her. Their place was up in the head of the Basin just across from where Swannie's place is now. Swannie had it torn down after Millard was gone. He didn't even leave the stones.

"Will and Millard were both ruthless businessmen. That's what Papa said. They kept others out of the basin by hook and by crook, using their water rights when they could and their muscle when they couldn't."

"What happened to Quackenbush, then? And where did Bert come from?"

"I was young at the time, so my recollection isn't terribly clear. I do remember Papa talking about the things that were going on. Both Will and Millard had visions of building the greatest ranch north of Texas. That was the way Montana would be built, they said. I remember Millard in

150

the store telling Papa that America would soon be the greatest nation on earth because of plain men having great dreams.

"But Will Johnson had the same dreams, and I guess they didn't feel they could pursue the same dreams on the same plot of land, so they became competitors. Enemies, really.

"In time Swannie began helping his father run the ranch, and somehow they were able to take over much of the Flying P herd. Millard accused them of stealing it, but he died before he could challenge what they had done."

"How did he die?"

"I never really knew, though I remember some men in the store saying he was crushed by the weight of his own ruthlessness. We heard every kind of opinion here in the store."

"And what became of him?" Chance said. "Where is he buried?"

"That I don't know. Mama and Papa didn't talk about it."

"Weren't there any kin? Didn't he have children or anyone to take the place over?"

"I never knew that, either. His wife died when I was quite young. But you know, I do remember something about a son in school somewhere. I remember that now. I think he even came to Montana one time. I can't remember whether it was during the summer one year, or at the height of the trouble, or what the circumstances were, but I never saw him. I only remember Mama and Papa talking about that one time. I'm sorry," she said. "My memory of all that is poor."

Chance was glad for what she had remembered. Ruthless or not, it seemed that Millard Quackenbush had seen his ranch stolen by the Johnsons while his heir was away at school—studying, no doubt, poetry and Latin.

"Was it ever your good fortune to know a hand in these parts called Toejam?" he asked.

151

The children giggled and Walter Hawkins guffawed. Maggie could not restrain a laugh of her own.

"I beg your pardon?" she said.

"Yes, ma'm. Toejam Early. I reckon he worked at one time for Will Johnson."

"I'm sorry, Mr. Chance. I'm sure I would remember. Could he be the relative you were asking about?"

The children laughed out loud now, along with Walter. Maggie pressed her fist against her funny lips.

Chance shifted in his chair. "Probably," he said. "Be my luck. But never mind that. Tell me the rest of what happened."

"After Mr. Quackenbush died, the Johnsons took control of the basin, and Will had his empire. It probably was the biggest ranch outside of Texas. About two years later he died and left it all to Swannie."

"So when did Bert move in? And how did he manage that if Swannie had the place sewed up so tight?"

"Bert came into the basin a short time after Will died. He challenged Swannie's claim to some of what Will had taken over from the Flying P, mostly water leases in the lower Basin, and the courts saw it his way."

"Swannie doesn't seem too fond of Bert, even today."

"No. He still believes Bert intends to take over the rest of the basin, just as his own father did before."

"There does seem to be some stock missing. From both sides. What do you hear about that?"

Maggie rose. The children did the same and began to clear the table. "Only rumors, Mr. Chance. There is stock missing, that seems to be a fact. The rest is just rumor. I teach the children not to set store by rumor."

Chance insisted on washing the dishes while the children went off to their studies. He recruited Walter Hawkins to help.

Maggie protested. "I won't have a guest in my own home do my work," she said.

"I'm not much of a guest, I'm afraid, just an ordinary ranch hand who would be washing someone else's dishes if I wasn't doing it here."

While he washed he asked about her husband. Tom Dark had died for no known reason in his sleep.

"He was a good man," she said.

"I'm sorry," Chance said. "I didn't mean to open up old hurts."

She put her hand to her mouth again for a moment. "That's all right," she said. "He was a good man, and his memory gives us strength."

"I believe you-all honor him right well," Chance said.

Maggie Dark smiled, a sad but lovely smile, and Chance believed he had never seen prettier.

The afternoon began to lengthen. Chance said goodbye to Maggie and her family and left. He swung the appaloosa up the street past the church and out of town on the Rocking Tree road. Just past the edge of town he left the road and turned east toward the river. He was not needed at the bunkhouse until Tuesday—and he had some other questions to answer before then.

XXII

THE GREAT HILLS OF THE SALLY BASIN SHIMMER IN the east as vast and still as a dream. But the world is a mystery of shadows and shifting light; in the contoured glow of sunset those same hills seem at once to recede into the distance and to loom toward the approaching night.

Chance made camp by a stream not far from the draw where he had found Black Moses. He didn't know what he expected to find. He got up early and at first light crossed the grassy arm into the draw. The carcass of the roan was gone, scattered by the scavengers of those hills.

All the tracks from Chance's last visit were gone as well, washed away by showers and erased by the wind. No new tracks had taken their place. Chance was alone.

A heavy dew had soaked the grass of the canyon. From the middle of the canyon near the creek, Chance could see that beyond the far thicket the canyon ended in a headwall split from top to bottom by a wide cleft, down which fell the creek. A man might climb out of the canyon by way of that cleft, Chance thought, but not a horse. Yet there had to be a way.

To the left of the thicket a granite rib descended from a slope above the canyon. Between the rib and the thicket a clearing of grass and stone ran back to the talus and the base of the wall. Chance rode into the grassy opening and around the foot of the rib.

Behind the rib a slope of sand and scree rose about forty feet to the mouth of another draw, much narrower than the canyon but broad enough for cattle. The draw appeared to climb toward a rift in the hills—and cattle sign dotted the slope.

Chance was pleased with himself. He had found the key to one of his mysteries—and possibly two or three. Two or three mysteries. He wondered for a moment if he weren't really pursuing an infinite progression of mysteries.

"I wouldn't be surprised," he muttered.

He spurred the appaloosa up the slope and into the draw above. The draw rose gently to a narrow bend about a hundred yards beyond, then opened out beyond the bend and continued to rise between the hills.

The gully was arid and still, but large numbers of cattle had been driven that way. He followed the gully as it rose toward the east, scanning the skyline above him for company. Grass was sparse among the sage and tumbleweed, and the breathless air grew stifling as the sun climbed into the sky. Behind him the Sally Basin was completely gone, as lost to him now beyond the hills, it seemed, as everything else about the past. Chance took his time.

The gully ended in a saddle well to the east of Sally Basin. Below him lay a high valley, down which a stream ran northward, probably to the Missouri. Meadows lined the valley and aspen lined the creek, while spruce and fir stood here and there in groves.

Chance dismounted to stretch his legs and let the horse blow. The route of the cattle trail he was following was no

155

longer clear. He would have expected it to turn northward down the creek, but from where he stood the valley looked much too steep.

He checked the cinches and mounted up. Just then something whirred past his head and spattered off a rock a few feet away as a shot split the air above him. Chance wheeled the horse and bolted down the trail as if they themselves had been fired from some great weapon. Three more shots echoed in the gully before they pulled out of range.

At the mouth of the gully they started down the slope. Just before they reached the bottom, another shot cracked ahead of them in the canyon. Chance kicked the horse down the slope and across the grassy patch into the thicket—the one where Black Moses' crossbreed bull had sought refuge from the cannons of the *Maine*. He hoped there were no cannons out there now.

He realized as soon as he swung out of the saddle that something was wrong. For a moment he was not sure what it was. His head hurt and the thicket began to dance.

He caught himself against a tree and tried to collect his wits, and at last it dawned on him that he had been shot. He checked himself and found a long wound on his side, bleeding and open to the ribs.

He thought he was safe for the moment. The shot seemed to have come from the rim above the head of the canyon, so he could take cover in the thicket—at least for a time.

His head began to spin again, but he told himself with grim humor he had survived that before. He tethered the appaloosa to a tree and pulled his bedroll from the animal's back, then, clutching the rifle, lowered himself into the grass among the trees and waited for the shock to pass.

He fell into a kind of half-sleep. When he emerged, he

could not tell how much time had passed. The sky was still bright. The canyon was quiet.

At least he was still alive. He had lost some blood, but did not think he had lost much. And some of the wooziness had left. He took his new shirt from his bedroll and dressed the wound as well as he could.

He sat with his back against a tree, much as he had before, when he had been out in the canyon and the menace there in the trees. He dozed again for a few minutes, then woke with a start, afraid that sleep might bring its baneful brother.

As he waited for night, dark clouds drifted in overhead, and began to rain. They rained lightly at first, then a little harder, then harder still. He managed to get his slicker on, but he was growing cold. He began to shiver, and the shivering made the wound ache all the more.

He sat against his tree and watched the meadow and the mouth of the draw. The meadow was peaceful in the rain. He inhaled, and in spite of the pain in his side, savored the cool, fresh air.

Behind him, at the base of the wall, a falling rock clattered against the talus and bounded into the thicket. Chance fumbled for the Winchester in his lap and rolled to his left, onto the wound. It seemed to start bleeding again, but for the moment he had other things on his mind.

He could not see the upper sections of the wall. Along the bottom and up the cleft of the creek he could not see anything out of place. He crept forward a little but could not see much more.

He crept back through the thicket and peered out. The meadow was quiet in the rain.

Chance knew he had to watch the meadow. A man could get down the headwall, but that did not seem likely, especially in the rain. All Chance could do was watch the meadow. Watch and listen.

157

He spent the afternoon like that—watching, shivering, and wanting to leave. As evening came he began to think he might be alone. The pain in his side became an ache that grew as he shivered. He thought a rib had been broken; one or two had been nicked for sure.

He shifted his legs a little and looked around behind him. He knew he was lucky to be alive. The rain continued, more softly than before. The patter of the rain and the falling of the creek were the only sounds in the canyon. Chance watched and waited as the light began to fade.

As soon as he could no longer see the wall across the meadow, he raised himself to his feet. His legs were stiff and weak, but he limped to the horse with the help of some trees.

He got himself into the saddle with difficulty as the thicket danced and swayed.

He tried to picture the meadow in his mind. He was north of the creek. He crouched in the saddle and started out of the trees. The features of the meadow were barely visible through the rain.

They crossed the stream, then kept to the trees near the place he had found Moses. The patter of the rain helped cover the sounds the horse made moving over the uneven ground. There was no sign of anyone else in the canyon. Chance realized that the patter of the rain would cover their sounds, too.

At the mouth of the canyon he dismounted. He took the carbine and started the horse alone down the draw, then circled to his right into the rocks. His legs began to wobble again. Sweat drenched his shirt and he began to shiver, and he thought he felt his side start to bleed again. He found a place where he could watch the draw, and sat down to let the dizziness pass.

There were no shots as the horse nosed his way down

the draw. Chance rested among the rocks until the horse was out of sight, but when he got up again everything began to spin. He picked his way out of the draw and found the horse. The rain let up, but he continued to shiver as he clung to the saddlehorn and started for the Rocking Tree.

He clung to his bunk for two days with the chills and the shakes and the spinning he thought he had left behind. Two ribs had been nicked, but nothing broken.

Fil Hazzard looked in on him at the bunkhouse and offered to bring the doc back any time Chance felt he was taking a turn.

"We need to get you healthy," he said. "Bert wants to pay you while you're laid up." He shook his head. "Bert's too easy. I don't know what this world is coming to. We need to get you healthy."

Within a week Chance was back on his feet, not strong but getting around. One Sunday he was playing cards with four other hands in the bunkhouse when Simon Wheeler came in from town.

"Feller asking for you in town," he said to Chance.

"That right?" Chance said.

"At the Slaughter House bar. Says he's looking for a low-down Texas shit-in-the-grass named Chance. Blood in his eye, too. I didn't tell him nothing, but he'll find out soon enough. He described you good, Chance, and said if anyone runs into you to tell you he'll be staying at the Slaughter House."

"Well, I'll be," Chance said. "Who is this gent? Did he say?"

"Curly-haired fella, from down Wyoming way. Said his name was Bagley."

XXIII

EXCEPT FOR ELIZABETH, BEAN BAGLEY WAS Chance's only friend. Chance could hardly imagine why Bagley was looking for him now, especially if Wheeler had read him right. He did not think he had, but he sensed that something was about to emerge from a time that was already becoming his past.

He had not yet returned to his place in the rotation, so Fil Hazzard gave him the okay to ride to town. He collected his bedroll and started for town.

The Slaughter House stood just up the street from the mercantile, across from the Moosehead Saloon, dark and gaunt under its steep Montana roof. Its interior added nothing to its glamor. The lobby was a small room just off the foot of a flight of narrow stairs. Opposite the lobby an unlit hallway led past the stairs to the rear of the hotel. Near the mouth of the hallway a dutch door opened onto the manager's apartment and served, when it was open, as the desk.

The manager was a short and flabby man with a shining expanse of cranium between fringes of dark hair. He wore a kind of permanent leer on his face.

160

"Afternoon," Chance said.

"What can I do for you?" The man's voice was that of a malevolent houserat.

"I reckon you have a guest named Bagley."

"All right."

"Tell me if he's in?"

"He's not," the manager said. "He went out a couple hours ago."

"Say when he'd be back?"

"Didn't say."

"Waal, my name is Chance. I understand he's been asking around for me."

The man's leer brightened measurably.

"Why yes, he has. Left word for you to wait. Seemed pretty emphatic."

"And you don't know where he's gone?"

"Sorry, he just said to have you wait in town. He's said that every day since he's been here."

"How long has that been?"

"Well, a couple days," the manager said.

Chance took a room. He knew he wouldn't be going back to the Rocking Tree that night in any event. Then he went next door to the Slaughter House Saloon. Compared to the establishment across the street, the Slaughter House Saloon was small and drab. The place was empty.

"Afternoon," he said to the bartender.

"Afternoon. What'll it be?"

"A little early yet. My name is Chance. I'm told a newcomer has been asking around for me."

"Ah, yes," the bartender said, "fella named Bagley. Staying here, I reckon."

"Seen him today?"

"No, he ain't been coming in till after supper. Probably be in tonight."

"Say what he wants with me?"

161

"Well, now, he give me the sense that you and him go back some."

"Yes, a little. I just can't feature why an old saddle pard would show up here of all places asking after me like that. He didn't say?"

"Not much. Seems to be over something he figures you owe him."

"Well I'll be," Chance said, plowing the fingertips of a hand across his brow. "But he didn't say what?"

"No. I reckon he figures that's between you and him. Listen, though, if this is something where there's gonna be trouble, just you two keep it out of here, okay?"

"Well, I can't believe there's gonna be no trouble, not betwixt old Bean and me."

Chance didn't put the appaloosa up at the livery but tied him out behind the hotel, then walked across to the Moosehead Saloon.

"I understand there's been a waddie asking for me," he said.

"Newcomer," the bartender said. "Been a couple newcomers in here lately."

"Together?" Chance said.

"No, I don't think so. Fella's been asking for you, I reckon he's just a cowhand. The other one I don't like. Hard fella, two guns. Wild west toughguy. Calls himself Stanche. Vasner Stanche."

"Never heard of him. How long has he been around?"

"Come in here a couple weeks ago, then disappeared for two-three days. When he come back he had been riding pretty hard."

"Any idea what he's up to?"

"Some of the hands say he's been hired by Bert due to this rustling business. Some folks say he works for Swannie. Don't nobody seem to know. Lot of folks getting edgy with him around—edgier than before."

"And the other fella, Bagley?"

"Don't seem to have anything to do with Stanche. Come in a couple days ago asking for you. Kind of edgy himself. Seemed mighty anxious to find you. Staying across at the Slaughter House."

"You ain't seen him today?"

"No, not yet. You might check over at the hotel."

Chance stepped back into the street and decided to call on Maggie Dark. He found her at the store.

"Afternoon," he said. "I understand a fella's been asking for me."

"Yes," she said.

Bagley had told her little except that he was looking for Chance and was staying at the hotel. She knew nothing about the other stranger, though she had seen him once or twice.

Chance told her he had taken a room at the Slaughter House. They laughed a little about that.

"Say," he said to her then, "I have another question. Does anybody live over east of here? Anybody at all?"

"No," she said, gazing out the window. "Well, not right over east, not for two or three days. But, now, there is old Laszlo. His place is north and east, I'd say, east almost from the mouth of the basin, over along the hills, down the northern slope. Laszlo Pendragon. He's a good day's ride from here, probably more."

"He raise cattle over there?"

"Sheep. He's been over there for years, as long as I can remember. He comes to town every other month or so to trade. I can remember him coming in here when I was quite little. He was different, being a sheepherder and all. He was married to a Shoshone woman, but she died years ago. He's an old man now, lives over there all alone. He's probably lived over there for forty years."

"How did he survive the wars over there?"

"Aside from his Shoshone wife, the Indians said he had strong medicine. They respected him, I think, but they feared him too. They left him alone."

"Has he ever run cattle, or strictly sheep?"

"Oh, I don't think Laszlo would ever have anything to do with cattle, or with cattle people, really. He stays over there alone with his sheep as he always has."

A new idea began to play with Chance's mind.

"And you say he's been over there maybe forty years?"

"Yes—why, I hadn't thought of that! Of course! He's the man who could tell you the history of the basin. One of the funny things about him. He has always kept to himself, but he's always known more about the Sally Basin than probably anyone else, as if keeping himself apart gave him a chance to watch. Yes, he might be your man."

Chance thanked Maggie for the information. She said she would tell Bagley if she saw him that he was in town.

The only places in town to get a meal were the two saloons. Chance was troubled about Bagley but he walked back to the Moosehead and ordered a steak and coffee. When he was done he talked for a while with a couple of the cowhands who had come in to drink.

Everyone wanted to know why he had been shot. "Don't know why," he said. "Headhunters, maybe."

He was still uneasy and decided he would have a better chance of finding Bagley back at the hotel. He left the Moosehead and crossed the street. At the hotel he sat in the lobby for a while trying to read a week-old Denver *Post*, but he couldn't concentrate. He went up to his room, but was too restless to stay put.

He didn't know why Bagley had come. And he couldn't understand where Bagley might have gone. He knew he must have brought some news, and from the accounts of

Bagley's mood he knew it wouldn't be good. He didn't want to think about that; he had enough on his mind already. But he had a growing sense of foreboding, and his side hurt, and now his head began to hurt as well.

He went back down the stairs and asked the manager if he had seen or heard from Bagley. He had not.

He went into the bar. A couple of hotel guests were there. Three townsmen were playing cards and two cowhands were talking and drinking whiskey. He didn't feel like playing cards, and he didn't feel like talking.

He stepped up to the bar and put his foot on the rail.

"What can I get you?" the bartender said.

Chance didn't even blink. "Mr. Jack," he said.

The bartender put a glass on the bar and turned away to find the bottle.

XXIV

ETHYL ALCOHOL IS AN ORGANIC COMPOUND PRO-duced by the action of the protein zymase on certain sug-ars. It causes intoxication by bonding at the molecular lev-el with willing receptors in the nervous system.

Chance knew how things were even before he woke up; something was driving him toward a waking he did not want. He raised his head and everything began to spin.

He did not know where he was. It was dark, but he could tell he was in a room; what room it was he could not tell. He was lying fully clothed on a small bed. There was a knock at the door. He recognized the knock as that which had driven him to wake.

He sat up on the edge of the bed and held his head in his hands to stop the spinning. Another knock seemed to hammer at his skull.

"What!" he snapped.

There was no answer, only a sound of some kind at the door. Then another knock.

Chance stood up and shuffled toward the door. He felt awful, but he knew he could have felt much worse. He opened the door.

Maggie Dark stood in the hall. She did not come in.

"Mr. Chance," she said, "I'm afraid something terrible

has happened." She spoke softly, but something seemed to flutter in her voice.

"What is it?" he said.

"Your friend Mr. Bagley has been murdered."

Everything was still trying to spin around him, but Chance began to sober up at once.

"What?"

"He was shot down in the street just a few minutes ago. I heard the shots."

"Bagley!" he said. He wondered if this was just another whiskey nightmare.

"Someone said you must have done it. Everyone knows he was looking for you. They've gone for the sheriff."

Chance's mind was reeling. "Why are you telling me?" he said.

"I don't know. I just thought I should. I don't think you're the kind that would kill anyone."

"Thank you," he said. He started to kiss her on the forehead, but thought about his whiskey breath. "You better get yourself home," he said. "I don't want you involved."

She disappeared down the stairs and Chance turned back to his room to get his gear. Then he went down the stairs and down the hallway and out the back door.

He found the appaloosa and unhitched it. The spinning returned as he swung himself into the saddle, and he clung to the horn for a moment like a gnat in a whirlwind.

The horse knew something was wrong. He snorted and twitched his ears and wouldn't move. As the spinning began to settle, Chance kicked him into a trot and started up the alley away from the voices he now heard in the street.

Past the church he turned over to the road, then north toward the Rocking Tree. He had no plan, but he needed time to think. He remembered nothing of the earlier part of the night. It was clear that he had been drinking; how he had gotten back to his room was not clear at all.

167

He couldn't believe that Bagley was dead. His mind lurched as he tried to come to grips with that and ride at the same time. Bagley dead! Why had he even come? What had he been trying to tell him? Why had someone murdered him? And who?

Chance racked his thoughts trying to remember where he had been. He had to have been passed out when the shots were fired, but he didn't know if he could prove that. He wasn't even sure of it himself.

He rode at a canter. If everything Maggie had said was true, the sheriff would be sending someone after him. He sensed in his whisky-dimmed brain that running might only make things worse. But he was running anyway.

Chance saw that this could be the end of his stay in the Sally Basin. He wondered if his life in this place had ended this way before. But for now the important thing was to get some space between himself and the madness in that town.

The sky began to grow light as he rode, but neither his eyeballs nor his brain welcomed the light. He gagged on his own breath and fought his stomache's efforts to turn itself inside-out. And his side hurt.

He thought about going back. Maybe it was not too late to clear up the confusion, and he might even get himself a drink. Or at least a cup of coffee.

But he didn't turn back.

About halfway to the Rocking Tree he left the road and turned up a draw among the pines. He covered his tracks, then led the horse up into a talus slope that headed in a steep gully. He had no idea where he was going.

The top of the gully ended among walls. To the right, beyond some brush, Chance could see what appeared to be a broken ledge that angled around a corner and out of the gully. He tethered the horse to some brush and found a way to the foot of the ledge.

168

The ledge crossed a sloping face then turned the corner and opened onto a brushy shelf that led in turn into a hanging gully a little higher. The gully seemed to top out on a tree-covered ridge about three hundred feet above.

He went back to the appaloosa and led him through the brush and out along the ledge. The horse did not like it there, but twitched his ears and followed.

When they reached the upper gully, Chance mounted and rode. He stayed on rock as much as he could to avoid leaving a trail. Before long they left the gully and started up a forested ridge that rose due west into the mountains.

Chance watched his backtrail as he rode. There was no sign that anyone was coming.

Around midmorning he traversed off the ridge into a high valley. He stopped by a stream to let the horse blow and give his head a rest.

He looked around. The valley lay between the slopes of ridges that towered on either side. Parks and meadows separated stands of open forest across the valley floor, and the stream meandered gently among them.

Chance did not think he was being followed. He was tired and wanted to rest, but he wasn't sure he should stop just yet. His stomach had settled some, but his head had not and the wooziness came and went. He drank from the stream, then realized that he was hungry. He did not believe he had eaten since that steak at the Moosehead.

He still wanted a drink, but decided to settle for what he had. He had brought a few biscuits and some jerky, so he ate a couple of the biscuits with some of the stream water and began to feel a little better. He cursed himself for not having brought coffee.

He mounted up again and followed the stream.

By midafternoon he had wandered among the trees and meadows into the head of the valley. He decided to make camp.

The valley was open there and treeless, except for scattered groves of alpine fir. Peaks rose to the north and the south, but at its head the valley climbed to an open pass.

The meadow below the pass was flanked on the north by steep talus slopes, and on the south by the plunging stream. The opposite bank of the stream was lined with firs partly concealing a rocky slope that led to cliffs.

He decided to bivouac away from the stream. Near the top of the meadow he found a spot in front of a stand of firs. From there, with the stream a hundred feet or more to his right, he had a good view of the approach to his camp.

He laid out his bed just in front of the trees. He decided against building a fire; besides, he had nothing to heat. He filled his canteen at the stream, then sat back against a tree to eat some of the jerky.

The valley had been overtaken by shadow. The mountaintops stood in the afternoon sun like bronze warriors against the blue of the sky. A cool breeze touched the meadow and whispered in the tops of the trees.

Chance took it all in and tried to remember. It was not by luck that he had come to that valley. He had known the way.

Now he had two choices—to leave the country and never return, or to stay and try to clear himself. If he left, his reason for coming to Montana would be lost forever. If he stayed, he could find himself in deep cowsoil. With probably the same result.

He did not believe he had taken any hand in the shooting. But who? Why? The questions banged around in his skull like tin pans in an earthquake.

The hard day on the trail had done nothing to clear his thoughts. What he really needed now was sleep, but the din in his brain would not quit.

As he watched the valley one thought kept coming back to him: someone had killed Bagley in order to get at him.

But who? The face of Swanson Johnson hovered in his

170

mind, staring up at him from his plate as it had that night over supper. It had to be Swannie, he knew.

But Chance knew he did not know. If he wanted to know the truth, he had to go back. He didn't really even know if he was a suspect. Surely someone could explain that he had been passed out in his room when Bagley was shot. Maybe Maggie had misunderstood. Or maybe someone had sent her to flush him out. He blew into his fist. If that was true, how easily he had fallen for it.

He wondered if he should have left Wyoming. He sensed through the fog that Elizabeth had something to do with the reason Bagley had come to Montana, but he could not tell what that reason was; he could not or he would not. But he knew he could not go back to Wyoming until he was finished in the Sally Basin.

The fog; the goddamned fog.

He decided to stay put for a while; he needed to clear the fog from his brain. He didn't know whose side time would take, especially in the Bagley affair. No one would expect him back in the Sally Basin, not if they believed he had murdered Bagley for reasons that arose from somewhere else. No one, that is, but Swannie; Swanson Johnson might expect him back.

He started when he thought he heard voices down in the trees along the stream. Slowly he leaned forward to catch the sound a little clearer, but the only voice he heard was the rushing of the stream.

He checked his Winchester, then leaned back against his tree. He heard the voices again. This time he almost recognized them, though he could not make out their words. He looked around at his meadow, and at the mountains, and down the valley. He knew he had been there before. He closed his eyes to wait for nightfall and listen to the voices.

XXV

GLANCING ACROSS THE MEADOW CHANCE NOTICED something he had not seen before. Obscured in shadow at the base of a cliff beyond the creek gaped the mouth of a cave. His heart hammered like a fist as he crossed the meadow, toward the cave.

He paused at the mouth. The opening was wet and slimy, and a foul-smelling breeze puffed forth like a putrid breath. Something told him not to go in.

The cave was narrow but tall enough to let him walk upright. The passage descended into the dark, and Chance had to steady himself against the clammy wall.

He stopped when he heard the sound of a stream ahead, an underground stream, the voice of some underground stream. The sound had a lingering quality that told him he was approaching a cavern.

The chamber was large. Its floor was flooded with an eerie light that filtered down from unseen fissures in the rock above. The light was dim, but supported a kind of meadow there in the cave.

A murky creek flowed through a somber marsh and disappeared into darkness away to Chance's left. At the end of the cavern a thicket of pallid trees receded into shadow.

Chance thought he saw a movement in the thicket, and his heart began to pound again.

Ahead of him to the right, slightly higher ground appeared to allow passage around the swamp. Another thicket receded into the darkness along that side of the cave. Chance started toward that thicket through ghostly knee-high grass.

When he reached the thicket he looked again toward the other. Again he saw movement there, though still he could not tell what it was. Something waited there in the end of the cave. Something in the thicket.

He moved toward it. Fear rose in his throat like a hand. He saw the movement again, then saw through the gloom, standing just among the trees, something that appeared to be the form of a human person.

My father, he thought. *I've found my father.* But he knew then that the figure was not his father and was no man at all but a woman, dressed in some pale gown and watching him from the grove.

He could not understand why he would find a woman in such a place. Who was she? What was she doing there? She seemed to consider him for a time, but said nothing and made no move to step out of the trees into the open. At last she turned away and disappeared into the grove.

Something told him not to follow. He watched the trees for what seemed like an hour, but realized finally that he was alone.

He looked up into the depths of the starry night and shivered a moment in the mountain cold. Elizabeth. He knew now why Bagley had come. Elizabeth was dead. He didn't want to believe that. How could Elizabeth be dead?

"Find yourself," she had said. "Be happy. But don't come back." He remembered the terrible hurt she had carried inside, and understood now that Elizabeth was alone even in death.

173

And all for what? A mad dream, she had called it. He could not guess now where that dream might lead him; evidently not back to Wyoming. He wanted to send it to hell; he wanted to trade that dream for his friends.

He thought of another woman he had left, also in pursuit of himself. He tried to remember Starla's face in the night. He tried to think of Toejam and Several and Bagley. He even thought about Maggie Dark. He tried to picture their faces and couldn't.

But the dream remained. He could not turn his back on his quest, even now. One face lingered in his mind. The ghost who had come to him in Wyoming had been his father.

The water of the stream was cold and made his fingers ache as he filled his canteen. Across the meadow a marmot whistled in the blossoming light of daybreak. Chance walked back to his camp and was about to lead the appaloosa to the stream when he spotted a rider coming out of the trees at the bottom of the meadow. He picked up the Winchester and walked to the horse, where he waited, and watched the rider come.

He watched carefully; he could not tell if this rider was alone. And there was something about the rider, something he could not make out. He stood with his horse between the rider and himself, his carbine at the ready, and watched the brush and trees as the solitary figure came on.

It wasn't long before he discovered what it was that made this rider different. The man was no plain cowhand—this cowhand was black.

174

XXVI

BLACK MOSES WAS LOYAL TO SWANNIE, CHANCE believed, so the situation was clear.

"Hold up right there," Chance said. "We'll wait for the others."

"Ain't no others," Moses said, "so I believe I'll just come in and get down."

Chance levered a round into the chamber and stepped around the appaloosa. "I suppose you're here to take me back," he said.

"I wouldn't go back just now," Moses said. "I expect they on the trail while we talking."

"So you're telling me you're not with no posse?"

"That's what I'm sayin'—but a posse sho on its way."

"Well, dammit, I don't know how you found me or why you've come, but now you've led them to me sure."

"Excuse me, now, but I ain't left half the trail here you did, and if I could follow you here, they will too. You left a trail a chile could follow, specially them branch scratchings in the dirt by the road. That's how I knew where you had went."

"Well don't that take the cake?" Chance said. "All right, you're here. You might as well come up to camp."

They walked to the trees near Chance's blankets.

"Good thing you ain't got much of a camp," Moses said, "cause you gon' have to break it."

Chance stopped. "Is that so?" he said.

"Sho am," Moses said, "less you planning to host a neck-tie social right here today."

"All right, all right," Chance said, "but tell me why you're involved in this. Why are you here?"

"They's a thing or two I expect you ought to understand," Moses said, "and it's a pity I have to explain. First of all, I don't much keer for you. You a plain biggety fool, and a ugly one at that. But I owe you my life, and that's why I'm here."

"Biggety fool?"

"Texas white trash fool, since you ask. But I ain't come here to drag all that around. You done saved my life—least I can do is give you fair warning."

Chance looked down and toyed at a tuft of grass with his boot. "So they think I killed Bagley, do they?"

"Sho do. Mister Evers, he's got his self a posse, but they's talk of a hanging party as well."

"Why would they get so riled about the death of a stranger? It's not as if Bagley was one of their own. He meant more to me than to any of them. Why would they get up a lynch mob over that?"

"Someone fanning the flames. I don't know who, but it seem he want you out of the way."

"And what about you? Aren't you taking a mite of a risk joining me like this? If you get found out, how can you ever go back?"

"I told you, I owe you my life. That mean something to me even if it don't to you."

"And for that you'd risk your neck to save a cold-blooded killer?"

"Well, now," Moses said, "I ain't stupid. Happens I don't believe you killed that boy."

176

"And how do you figure that?"

"I was in town that night to get supplies for Mister Johnson. Now, they don't rightly 'llow no niggers in the Slaughter House, so I was sleeping in the rig as I usually do in town, just off the street by the livery barn. Jim Crow Hotel, I call it. That shooting done interfered with my rest, and as I looked out to see what was up, I seen that gun-totin' man Stanche a-slinkin' around the corner and out of sight. He damn near seen me, too, but he seemed to have his mind on getting his skinny butt offa that street."

"Then why the hell didn't you take that to Evers? Maybe they'd be looking for Stanche now and I could be getting a decent breakfast."

"Right away someone starts hollering 'Chance,' like they seen it too. This may be the West, but they still don't take the word of no nigger over that of a white man—specially after you took off the way you done."

"Who started the hollering, then?"

"I don't know, but pretty quick it was everybody."

"So Stanche shot Bagley in the dark," Chance said.

"Looked that way to me."

"But why?"

"Coulda been any reason. I don't guess he told me which one."

"I'll tell you what I think," Chance said. "I think it was a hired assassination. I think it was somebody trying to get at me without drawing attention to himself. I think they wanted to kill me and blame it on Bagley, but Bagley was gone when I came to town, so when they saw a chance to do it the other way around, that's what they did."

"You was shot up once already, wasn't you?" Moses said.

"That's right. Feels like someone's been stalking me. I don't suppose you know who."

Moses scowled. "I don't suppose it matter if I do," he said. "So suppose you tell me what I've got myself into."

177

"We'll have time for that later," Chance grumbled. "Seems to me we need to spend our energies right now getting the hell out of here."

"Sho nuff," Moses said. "You the boss."

"How well do you know these mountains?"

"I expect I know these mountains about as good as anyone. I been knowing this secret valley of yours for years."

"Then what do you suggest?"

"We can work our way out the Arrowhead yonder," Moses said, gesturing toward the pass above them. "They'll be watching for us down the Sally, but over to the Arrowhead we'll be able to ease out of this country and off in any direction."

"I'm not leaving this country," Chance said. "You go ahead. I appreciate what you've done for me, but I've still got business in the basin. I would surely admire if you could tell me a back way onto Big Grassy land."

"Big Grassy!" Moses did not seem to believe his ears. "What kind of business could you have there now?"

"Just some old interests I can't leave quite yet. Can you tell me a way?"

"Oh, they's a way, all right, but you ain't rid of me that easy. Duty binds, even if I don't like it no more than you, but I expect I'll want to know what this all about before you see Big Grassy land again."

"Dammit, now, you don't owe me . . ."

Moses cut him off. "I know you ain't gon' say 'nothin'," he said. "May not seem like much to you, but this man pays his debts."

Chance pushed his hat back a little. "All right," he said. "It don't matter to me. Do what you need to do. I'm going."

"You hear me, now," Moses said. "I aim to know this business of yours before you set foot on Grassy range again. I ain't gon' get drug into nothin' where I might have to take both sides at once. A man in that position could get plain touchy."

Chance understood him and realized he only had a few hours to decide how far to trust his surly new companion. He lashed his gear behind the saddle, then led his horse toward the pass. Moses followed.

The pass was steep, and mostly shale. The sun rose as they climbed; by the time they reached the top, they were all sweating hard.

They stopped in the pass to catch their breath. The air was thin at that height, and chilly in the breeze that swept the ridge.

Below them, over the pass, the valley of a creek descended northwest into the chasm of the Arrowhead. Beyond the river rose more peaks.

The pass itself was the low point in a ridge that connected the peaks flanking Chance's meadow. The pass was festooned with juniper and stunted fir, and the air was pungent with the scent.

Chance could not see the basin to the east, but far beyond the mouth of the valley rose those hills, dancing brown and yellow in the sun. Chance believed he could just make out that long, waterless draw he had discovered only days before.

There was still no sign below them of Moses' posse.

Moses picked up a piece of the shale that covered the pass and studied it as if hoping to learn something about shale. He turned it over in his hands a few times and brushed at it with his fingers, then seemed to give up. He drew back his arm and threw the stone toward the west, out over the creek and its canyon, over the slopes and the trees and the meadows that flanked the pass, over them all and down, down into the rocks below.

"Be a nice place to set a spell if you hadn't of dragged a hangin-posse after your tail," Moses said, wiping his hand on his jeans.

Chance was thinking of Elizabeth at the time.

179

"Sure," he said. "But I guess I did. Maybe we better light us a shuck."

The back side of the pass was gentler than the front. The slope there sprouted paintbrush and lupine, and the firs stood in little groves. The men had a long way to go into the valley of the Arrowhead, so with another look down their backtrail and out beyond the Sally, they mounted up and started down the slope.

They spent the rest of the morning working their way down the nameless creek. They stopped when they reached the river, a tumbling stream that looked like anything but a route into the mountains.

"Arrowhead," Moses said. "This here your chance to clear out of this country alive, and I shorely recommend you take it. I know you ain't killed that boy. This here your chance, and then we can be shut of each other."

"Go ahead," Chance said. "I don't mean to involve you in my problems, but I've got things to do."

Moses studied him for a moment, then looked at the rushing stream. "Have a hell of a time getting up this river," he said.

"Thanks for your help," Chance said. "I'll manage."

"Then you gon' have to manage me as well. Could be you'll come to regret that yet."

Chance mumbled something then started his horse into the river and turned upstream. Moses was right behind.

They rode and waded up the river, sometimes in strong, swift water, so they wouldn't have to come out onto the bank. They kept to the river in places where keeping to the river was hard, and they kept to the river in places where keeping to the river was bad. Chance wanted the posse to think they had gone downstream, and did not want to leave sign that they had not.

180

The day was beautiful. The smell of the river seemed to call up memories just beyond Chance's reach. Little eddies of oxygen and nitrogen wafted under the banks and carried cool fertile scents all along the water, the exuberant salamander smells of the river and the trees and the earth.

But even as Chance inhaled the breath of the river, the pale ghost of Elizabeth haunted his thoughts. He felt something oozing inside him as they climbed, something seeping and bleeding like a wound. He was glad the travelling was hard; it helped keep his mind from the thoughts and the seeping inside.

When they could follow the riverbed no more, they climbed into a rockslide on the far bank and led the horses three or four hundred feet up through the rocks.

They followed rock debris below some cliffs until they joined the river once more at a narrowing of the canyon. Above that spot the river leveled out in a long and open valley. They followed the riverbed again until they were overcome by exhaustion and night.

They camped in a low pass that Chance hoped led back to the basin on Big Grassy land. Moses wouldn't say. A flat little meadow occupied the pass with forage and water and trees, much larger than the trees on the pass they had crossed that morning.

They did not build a fire. They sat back against trees a distance apart and watched the clearing while they ate their meager rations in the dark. Beyond the branches overhead Chance could see a handful of the stars. In spite of everything, the place was peaceful as he sat. He wished he could have come another time.

Time, he thought. *A time to seek, and a time to lose.*

"Tell me what you done drug me into," Moses said across the distance.

181

"I ain't drug you into nothin," Chance said. "You're free to go."

"Sho," Moses said. "And you free to run for President."

"All right," Chance said. "Okay." He studied the branches and the stars. He appeared to be stuck with this man who would be Moses; he knew he had to tell him something, but he didn't know what.

He didn't know how far to trust him. So far he hadn't seen a single sign of anyone trailing them. Even if Moses was on the level, there was just too much he had no right to know.

"I'm too wore out to talk," Chance said at last. "I'll tell you what you want to know in the morning. Till then I'm going to get some sleep."

"I'll give you that," Moses said, "but we ain't leaving this meadow until I know what kind of business you have with Swannie."

"That's fine," Chance said. "I'll be out of your hair by daybreak."

"You miss my point," Moses said. "Till I know what I need to know, ain't nobody leaving this meadow."

Chance tried to calculate the prospects of getting free of Black Moses. It was a calculation he did not have the strength to make.

"I only need to know three things," Moses said. "I'll tell you now so you can think it over in your sleep. Don't worry yourself none about whether it's my business." He chuckled a little to himself in the dark under his tree. "No, too late for worrying about that now."

"So tell me the three things," Chance growled.

"Just three," Moses said. "Why are you here? Why do someone want to turn you to dust? And what is your business with Swannie?"

"I'll think about those," Chance said. "In my sleep. And I'll think about whether any of this is your business or not.

I may just decide to take my chances down the Arrowhead after all."

Moses flashed a grin Chance could see through the night. "Then maybe I'll just let you go," he said.

Chance rolled out his blankets under the cover of the trees. Moses picked his bedroll up and moved to a stand some hundred feet away: separate but equal. Now if they were discovered, they wouldn't be pinned down in one spot.

At least he doesn't expect me to sleep next to him, Chance thought.

XXVII

CHANCE LAY ON HIS BACK TRYING TO SEE THE SKY through the canopy of the trees. His side hurt. It had held up all right during the day and had not reopened, even in the water, but it hurt.

Yet something inside hurt much worse.

He thought again of the woman he had left. He thought of her as he had first seen her, and how she had awakened something in him even then. He thought of her in her white dress the first time he had dined in her absurd palace, and thought of her in the same dress the night he left, asking him not to go. He thought of the way she had laughed at his jokes and wondered with him about his past and touched his face. And he thought of the wan specter he had seen in hell.

He wanted to go back to her, to forget this madness and be with her and make things right again. He thought of the sharpness of her mind and the beauty of her spirit and the passion with which she had made love. And he thought of the way she had asked him not to leave.

Smoke, Several had called this. Madness. Believing that his past pointed to a future he could not ignore, maybe he had allowed that future to create the past on which it was built. And where had it brought him? He looked up through the branches.

Smoke. Madness. He had come because he had to.

He got up, then sat down at the tree where he had sat before and rolled a cigarette.

And he thought.

He jumped when a twig snapped behind him in the woods.

"Settin' up kinda late, ain't you?" That goddamn Moses.

"Too tired to sleep," Chance said.

"Too bad for us we ain't asleep. If we gon' leave this camp, we gon' have to leave it soon."

"And you need to know where I'm taking you. And why."

"If we gon' leave this camp."

"Tell me again about the three questions," Chance said.

"Suppose you tell me."

"I don't remember them."

"You told me you would think them over. You mean you lied?"

"I said I'd think about them in my sleep. I haven't been able to sleep. Something about me dragging you into something, right?"

"That's right. I want to know what you done drug me into and what's your business with Swannie."

"That's only two," Chance said.

"Never mind. It's enough for now."

"Sit," Chance said. "This may take some telling."

Moses sat and leaned back against a tree facing Chance. "Don't tell it too long," he said, "or it might end right here."

"How long have you lived in the basin?" Chance said.

"Long time," Moses said. "On and off twenty-five, twenty-seven years."

"*Damn*," Chance whispered, "is that right? Then you were here in the Flying P days?"

"Oh yes, for a time."

"And you knew Millard Quackenbush?"

185

"Can't say I knew him. Niggers wasn't sought out socially in them days."

"But you knew who he was. You knew about his ranch and all."

"About as much as any other Grassy hand."

"What happened to him? How did he lose it?" Chance's heart was thumping again in his weary ribs.

"That was a long time ago. What it got to do with you and Swannie?"

"I'm not sure," Chance said, "but we're coming to that."

"Well, Mister Quackenbush and old Mister Johnson was partners in the early days round here, but they divided up the basin and slowly begun to fall out with each other over the various jealousies old mens will have. Around 'eighty I done took and left the basin on wanderings of my own. When I finally come back, Mr. Quackenbush was gone, and his outfit with him.

"It hadn't been more than a few years or so, but Mr. Kaffo was already finishing his place down in the other end of the Basin."

"What happened to Quackenbush? Whatever became of him?"

"Murdered, I expect."

"By who?"

"I don't guess they ever did find out."

"Didn't he have a son somewhere? Someone that could have taken over the place?"

"Well, when I come back stories was flying about what really done happened. I never met no son myself, but somebody said Quackenbush had a son, away to school or somewheres. They said he had came home when he heard the place was in trouble and wanted to claim his birthright. He and the old man fell to disputation and the son up and killed him—his own daddy—and laid the

186

blame to someone else. Then he left the territory and was never heard from in these parts again."

A queasy chill spread among Chance's insides. "Is that what happened?" he said.

"That was just one of the stories. Another was that there was actually two sons. One come when he heard the place was in trouble, then went off again for help. Then the second one come in here and killed the old man or whatever."

"Two sons? And what became of them?"

"Never heard. Well, now, I heard one time that the sons done caught up with each other and one of them killed the other. But that's all just stories. I cain't tell you what happened. There was even stories that Swannie was the one who done killed Mr. Quackenbush or that he had someone to do it for him. Don't nobody really know—all depend on what you want to hear."

"Have you ever heard of a man called Laszlo Pendragon?"

"Sho. Everybody know Laszlo."

"How well do you know him?"

"Don't nobody know Laszlo well. But he know them. Mm, mm, ain't that the truth. I expect he getting old by now."

"Would he know what really happened?"

"Might. Might at that. Not much Laszlo don't know."

"And he lives over east of the basin?"

"East and north. He live down to the foot of them hills beyond the badlands."

"How far from here, would you say?"

"Two days. But you still got a sight of explaining to do right here, and we running out of time."

Chance couldn't conceive of a way to explain his intentions without explaining the whole reason he was there. He knew Moses would never take him to Swannie until he was satisfied he knew the truth—and he knew Moses would never let him go alone.

He thought about Elizabeth and felt the seeping inside,

187

then looked at this tough dark man through the night.

He explained about his drinking and his memory and about meeting an old man who told him he might be Quackenbush's long lost boy.

"Ever know a man called Toejam?" he said.

Moses made a noise like the quacking of a duck, a sort of laugh he had. "I expect I'd remember," he said.

"Well, in any case, I came here to find out if he was right. That's all. Then I stumbled onto something that looked like the rustling everyone's so exercised about, and now someone wants me out of the way—for one reason or the other. I still don't know which. But I believe Swannie recognized me the other night, and I aim to find out."

Black Moses watched him as he spoke, the whole of his lower face hidden in a massive hand. He moved his hand and took a breath. "So which son are you," he said, "the good one or the bad?"

"Maybe that's what I've really come to find out."

"And what about the dead man in town?"

"A friend of mine with bad news," Chance said. "Whoever wants me tried to get me through him."

"And you think Swannie that man."

"I don't know." Chance watched Moses in the dark, partly to read his reaction and partly because he could not look away.

"And what do you aim to do once you've done cornered him in his den?"

"I don't know that, either. I guess I expect to stare him down, about the way you're doing to me right now, and find out leastwise if he knows who I am."

"And if he do?"

"I don't know."

"And you want me to let you ride down there in the night to a man who ain't never done nothing by me but right and let you face him down in his own home about a past twenty years dead and gone."

188

"I guess that sizes 'er up," Chance said.

"A past that could yet have another killin' or two in it," Moses said.

"No, I don't want that. But I have to find out. I've put everything on this and I'm afraid I intend to find out."

"I can see that," Moses said, "but I don't like it. Cain't no good come of letting a man like you just slip into Swannie's home by night for no kind of showdown. Lord, no. And how you know you gon' find out what you want that way anyhow? You be better off to find Laszlo first and learn what you need from him, then come back and face Swannie if you must."

"I've thought about that," Chance said. "But I'm here now, and I may never get another chance to talk to Swannie. Once I leave this basin, what's the chance I'll ever get near Swannie Johnson again?"

"'Bout the same as it is right now. I'm sorry, but I cain't let you go down there for no midnight showdown."

"Then you'll have to kill me yourself, 'cause otherwise I'm going."

Moses watched him through the dark.

"You ain't bluffin', is you?"

"What have I got to lose?" Chance shrugged a little in answer to his own question.

Moses watched him, saying nothing as he thought. "All right," he finally said. "I ain't killin' nobody, yet. But you need to know one thing sho: I ain't bluffin' neither. Anything happen to Swannie, you one dead fool, I don't care whose life you done saved."

"I know you mean that," Chance said through the night.

"You damn right I do. I'll take you to him, but I'm stickin' witch you—and you holding your life in your hands."

"I won't do anything to Swannie," Chance said. "And I'm not dumb enough to mess with a man who talks like you."

"I know you ain't," Black Moses said.

The men rode out of the mountains in the night. "Where was the Flying P?" Chance asked. Among some trees between the mountains and the river Moses showed him the site. In the moonlight the clearing was as still as a graveyard. "Nothin' left," said Black Moses.

Chance ignored Moses' proddings to get moving. He lingered in the clearing for a moment as the horse grew impatient. Nothing was familiar. Nothing came back to him.

They crossed the river. The buildings of the Big Grassy lay sprinkled like fragments among the shadows of the moon. The men skirted the buildings to a place in the trees just west and a little north of the main house. Morning was only a couple of hours away. Chance had to get in to see Swannie quickly and get out again if he hoped to be out of there before the ranch began to stir. He knew he could be walking into a trap, but that was the chance he had to take.

They dismounted by a stand of pines about fifty yards from the house. They tethered their mounts to trees and approached the back of the house. Moses walked with a limp, yet he moved like a phantom through the night; twice Chance had to look back to be sure he was still there.

The back of Swannie's house rose between the men and the sky. A gentle breeze carried the scent of pine down from the mountains. An early catbird mewed in a tree to their right.

At the foot of the steps Chance paused and whispered to Moses. "Cover me from here," he said, "and keep an eye on the horses."

"Cover your own damn self," Moses whispered. "I'm sticking witch you."

Chance whispered something more, mostly to himself, then started up the steps.

The granite steps didn't make much noise, but the porch was another matter. The decking seemed to have been laid like the skin of a drum. Chance crept toward the kitchen door with the care of a man crossing dangerous ice.

Moses stuck to Chance like a shadow, his shooting iron now in his hand.

Chance eased the door ajar and slipped in. Moses moved in silently behind, then tugged on Chance's sleeve. "You wait in the parlor," he whispered. "You mind you, no monkey business. I'll get Swannie and bring him down—I ain't letting you up there alone. You best pray I don't wake Elroy. Elroy find us here, there'll be hell to pay." He held out his hand. "Here," he said. "Let me have your gun."

Chance almost spoke out loud. "*What?*"

"You heard me," Moses said. "Cough it up, or this meeting over before it start."

Chance drew his weapon and handed it to Moses in the dark.

They moved into the parlor. Then Moses stole up the staircase, his own weapon still in hand. At the landing he looked back at Chance, then disappeared up the steps.

Within two minutes Swanson Johnson was coming down the stairs. He wore only his underwear, but carried his pants over one arm. He glowered at Chance; at the foot of the stairs he put on the pants.

Moses patted Chance quickly with one hand while he held his weapon in the other. "You ain't picked up no guns, is you?" he said softly. Chance shook his head. Moses lit a lamp on a small table beside one of the chairs, then motioned the two men to sit. "Swannie," he said, "Mr. Chance have a few questions he need to ask. I'll let you gentlemen talk. But mind," he said to Chance, "I'll be right here, and you under the gun."

Swannie glared as Moses disappeared into the darkness of the kitchen. "What do you want?" he said.

"Somebody has murdered a friend of mine," Chance said, "and I aim to find out who."

"A friend of yours?"

191

"That's right. Somebody wants me out of the way and it looks like they figured they could use that fella Bagley in town. But I guess they didn't figure, with Bagley bad-talking me so, that we were friends. I don't aim to be framed, Swannie, and I don't aim to let my pardner's killers go."

"And you believe I know something about it."

"I believe you know quite a few things it has become my business to know."

"What are you up to? Why have you come here?"

"You recognized me the other night, didn't you?"

"What are you talking about?"

"Don't play dumb with me, Swannie. You know who I am, I saw it in your eyes. You weren't quite sure at first, but you know."

Swannie's eyes studied Chance from under those dark brows much as they had that night.

"All I know about you," Swannie said, "is that trouble seems to go wherever you go, and we have enough trouble here without you. I don't know what you think you're going to get out of me but I don't know anything about your friend, so why don't you clear out of here while you still can and leave us alone?"

"Might be a good idea to hold your voice down," Chance said. "I don't want anyone else getting hurt over this. You know a lot more than you're letting on, and I intend to reach some kind of understanding."

Swannie pulled at his nose and looked Chance straight on. "I can't tell you but what I know."

"Then tell me about Stanche. How long has he worked for you?"

"The gunslinger? He's not mine, I don't hire gun slingers. I told you, we have enough trouble here already. How stupid do you think I am?"

"I know Stanche isn't here for the waters. And I know he doesn't work for Bert. It's going to come out, Swannie—we

192

might as well get it out now."

"And what does he have to do with this?"

"There were witnesses to the killing. At least one that I know of. All I have to do is dodge your lynch party for another day or two and everybody in the basin will know who really killed Bagley."

"You're saying Stanche killed your friend for me?"

"That's the way she looks, and there's only two reasons I can think of. One is the rustling. I got kinda close to that the other day, and someone didn't like it. Your man Stanche, I'd say. The other is the Flying P. I don't guess anybody knows much about that any more."

Swannie's voice rose again as he spoke.

"The Flying P! That was a dead issue long before Bert dredged it up again."

"But it's kinda come back, hasn't it?

Swannie stared at Chance. "I know who you are," he said. "But you must be insane. What do you want?"

"All I want is the truth," Chance said.

"The truth! Well that beats everything! Here's the truth— Bert Kaffo is a crooked son of a bitch who plans to steal the rest of the Sally Basin just the way he's stolen what he has now. You should be talking to Bert and Fil about this man Stanche. I have nothing to do with him."

Chance studied Swannie's face for signs of truth or signs of falsehood. Or signs of anything at all.

Just then he caught a movement on the stairs and bolted from his chair. Elroy was coming down the stairs, gun in hand.

"Moses!" Chance barked as Swannie sprang from his chair as well.

Suddenly the place was on fire. A finger of flame ran across Swannie's polished floor to the lace curtains by the windows, and climbed the curtains like a waterfall turned upside down. Flame took over Swannie's parlor as sud-

193

denly as if some force, some energy, some vengeance or horror had waited all those years for the moment it would be unleashed as fire.

The parlor was dark now except for the light of the flames. Gunshots exploded as thick smoke began to fill the place and Swannie sprinted up the stairs for his wife. In an instant the house had become a bedlam of chaos and madness.

Chance found Moses in the kitchen door and ran into the yard. Elroy fired after them, then began ringing the bell as Chance and Moses reached their horses, already rearing against the tethers.

"What did you do in there?" Moses shouted.

"Nothing. Elroy came down the stairs and all hell broke loose."

Moses was first up on his mount. He still held his weapon in one hand while he tried to control the horse. Chance's appaloosa wanted to bolt; they struggled in a grotesque cotillion as Chance tried to mount.

"Why you started that fire?" Moses demanded, his revolver now bobbing in the direction of Chance's head.

"I didn't do it. I think Swannie knocked over the lamp." He swung up into the saddle.

Moses kept his weapon on Chance while he wrestled with his horse, then holstered up. "We best ride," he said grimly. "Be more trouble than help around here."

Behind them the whole ranch sprang to life. Men appeared everywhere as a bucket brigade formed a futile queue. The house was fully involved; flames licked from the windows and began to spread along the roof. Chance and his reluctant deliverer melted into the night as the flames leaped into the sky.

XVIII

THE MEN RODE NORTHWARD ALONG THE FOOT OF the hills. Behind them a column of smoke still rose from the basin to a height of several hundred feet, where it flattened out like a toadstool in an upper wind. A smoky haze was beginning to fill the basin and tinge the morning sky.

They had ridden east and a little south from the burning ranch as if to disappear into the Big Grassy mountains, then had mingled with a herd to cover their tracks and turned north along the hills.

They knew the smoke would draw riders from everywhere in the basin, so they rode with the thought of drifting into the hills if anyone came into sight. They still saw no sign that they were being followed.

Black Moses was now completely caught up in Chance's erratic odyssey—the fire had changed everything.

Chance told him what he knew. "The canyon where I found you runs east through a notch clean into the hills. I don't think most folks know that. Unless they're laying for us there, we ought to be able to slip out of the basin that way. They'll damn near certain be watching for us every other way."

"Likely."

"And that's where your disappearing stock has been disappearing to. I staggered up there the other day with my backside flapping in the breeze, but I expect a couple more cautious *hombres* could poke around up there and learn a thing or two without getting shot."

"You don't think whoever up to all this will be watching for you there too?"

"Oh, they might, if we give them time to beat us there. But maybe not. I still like our odds better up that way than anywhere else."

"And what do you expect to find?"

"I don't know. Cattle, maybe. Sign. Even rustlers. Maybe someone that'll talk. But even if we don't find anything, that way should take us as good as any to where we're going."

"To Laszlo."

"You say he lives over that way?"

"More or less. North some."

"But we could get there that way?"

"I expect, if we can stay clear of all them rustlers."

About two miles from the Big Grassy line shack they turned up a draw that took them out of the basin and into the yellow hills. Once they were out of sight of the basin they turned north again toward the trail that had first brought Chance into that country.

They believed the trail would be watched. From the brow of a hill they had a good look along the trail, but no one was there.

"If anyone watching," Moses said, "they probably down where the trail narrow to follow that ridgeline into the badlands."

"What would keep us from sticking to the hills until we reach that pass where I was fired at?"

"Probably not much," Moses said. "A creek come out of there, could have a canyon or whatnot, but it got to have water, too—something we gon' need before this day over. I cain't believe we got much to lose by finding out."

They descended a slabby area to the trail, which they crossed at a rocky place. They kept to the rocks and followed the spine of the hills toward the north.

Near evening they dropped into Moses' creek. A spring fed a marshy pond in a little fold among the hills, and the pond fed a stream that drained to the east. The men decided to stop for the night.

"I could use some rest," Moses said.

"And some food," Chance added. "I'm fresh out. I reckon game will be using this here watering hole. You got any snare line?"

"Oh, I got better than that." Moses dismounted and reached into a saddle bag. He brought out a canvas sack and held it up. "From Swannie's pantry," he said. "He owe me some pay anyhow."

They ate a meal of bread and canned corn. Moses had also brought a slab of bacon, but they did not want to light a fire. No one suggested eating it raw.

"Maybe after tomorrow," Moses said.

"Sure," Chance said. "But damn, I wish we had some coffee."

"And what would you do with it? Suck on the beans?"

"I've sucked on worse," Chance said.

They ate in silence for the few minutes they needed to finish off the meal.

"Mm, mm," Moses said. "Good. Lip smackin' good."

"Lip smackin'," Chance said.

Moses finished scraping out the can, then stood up and flattened it with the heel of his boot. "Well," he said, "I believe I'll backtrack a piece and see what cookin'."

Chance got up. "I'll go with you," he said.

"Don't matter," Moses said.

They mounted and started back up the hill. They doubled

back on their trail by angling toward the west-breaking slope. They dismounted by a stand of pines near the crest and approached the top on foot.

"Mind you watch for snakes now, you hear?" Moses said. "They'll just be heading for home."

Chance stopped. "Snakes!" he said. "I'm from *Texas*, for God's sake. You think I never saw a God-damn *snake*?"

Moses made a sound in his throat. "Just you mind," he said.

The top of the hill was a rocky outcrop from which they had a view of the basin and could see back down their trail for miles. No one was in sight.

The hill to the north, beyond their little pocket, rose several hundred feet higher than the one where they stood, but everything else lay below. The hills were bathed in the purple shadows and gold light Chance had seen his first evening in those parts.

Moses squatted and picked up a stone, much as he had the day before in the mountains across the way. They could not see those mountains now; a shroud of smoke hung over the basin.

Chance sat down where he could see in almost every direction. A bird called out from the grass to his right—a lovely birdcall of evening. He did not know what kind of bird it was. Nothing else broke the silence of those hills.

"Lord, Lord, Lord," Moses said softly as he looked out over the basin, "what have we done?" He studied the stone a turn or two then tossed it out in front of him a few feet and looked at Chance. "You know you ain't out of the woods yet on this Swannie business."

Chance heaved a sigh. "No, I don't expect so," he said.

"I ain't rightly satisfied with what happened back there. There wasn't no damn fire in the bargain."

"You were there. You saw what happened."

"That don't make it right," Moses said, "and I ain't satisfied and you ain't out of the woods."

The two men watched the hills again in silence.

"Well," Chance said at last, "I suppose if one of us is going to keep watch, this ought to be the place."

"You go ahead and watch if you want to," Moses said. "I'm so damn tired I don't much keer if they ketch us or not."

Chance paused. "I suppose you're right," he said.

Moses plucked a long stalk of grass and put the end of it in his mouth. "So what's your next move?" he said.

"How well do you know these hills?"

"A little," Moses said, "but not good. Don't nobody ever come up here."

"Could be trouble ahead, as well as behind. How good are you at keeping your head down?"

Moses made his little throat sound once again. "Five years I scouted for the U.S. Army," he said. "I ain't lost this old scalp yet. That make me good enough to travel with you?"

"You scouted for the Army?" Chance said.

"Tenth Cavalry, Fort Davis, Texas, Colonel Benjamin Grierson. Damn fine officer, Colonel Grierson."

Chance just blinked. He didn't know whether he had ever heard of such a thing. "But how . . . ?"

Moses took the grass from his mouth and held the stalk between his fingers and his thumb. "Grew up in Tennessee," he said. "Cut a boy there when I wasn't no more than a boy myself. Damn near killed him, too. Long time ago. I don't keer to think about it much any more, but it was enough to set me hankering to seek my fortune in the West.

"I knew how to ride a mule, so I stole me a horse and rode it to the panhandle. Last thing I ever stole—till lately, anyway." He looked at Chance and let the flicker of a smile cross his face.

"I worked as a cowhand there for a time, but Texans ain't always been too well disposed toward colored folks, as I expect you know." He looked at Chance again.

199

"I guess I heard that somewhere," Chance said.

"So I drifted up into Colorado and worked there four-five years, mostly as a horse wrangler for the Army. I met a man named Malachi Flood, who trapped and hunted and scouted some for the Army. He taught me scouting. That was when I learned about the colored regiments of the U.S. Cavalry. They even had a unit of half-nigger Injuns for scouts. That fired my imagination some.

"About 'seventy-six I come to Montana and went to work for old Mister Johnson. He had just finished building that fine stone house we've done burned down. I worked here four years or so, then took on with the Colored Tenth in 'eighty as a wrangler. And I be damn if they didn't set me to scouting, onliest pure nigger scout in Texas at the time, I expect.

"So that's it. In time I give up scouting Injuns and left Texas for good."

"And you came back to herding cattle instead of red folks."

"Well, not straight off. I moved to Saint Joe Missoura and took up preaching the Gospel of the Lord."

"The Gospel! So you're a preacher, are you?"

"I was, yes indeed. I expect I was a damn fine preacher, too."

"Well, I'll be. So what brought you back to Montana?"

"Just got tired of city life. Couldn't stand that city livin'. Fifteen years I been back. When I left, there was Mr. Johnson and old Mr. Quackenbush's Flyin' P. When I come back it was Swannie and Bert. Swannie took me back on, and now you've done burned that fine old place right down." Moses fell silent again as he looked again up the basin.

Chance began to sense in this man something of the wanderer he had discovered in himself.

"What about family?" he said. "Did you ever marry? Children?"

200

Moses took the stalk of grass from his mouth once more and studied it for a moment the way he had studied the stone. Then, as he had done with the stone, he threw it down the hill, chewed end first.

"Oh, yes," he said. "Yes indeed. Married a young gal in Saint Joe. Sarah Emerson, she was. Fine young gal."

Moses plucked another stalk of grass and chewed the end, looking down the hill as if looking down the years of his life.

"What happened?"

"She tried to give me a son there in Saint Joe but the boy, he died being born. I never even gave him a name. Church folks, they gave him a fine burial in the colored cemetery in Saint Joe, but they buried him without ary a name.

"Sarah, she took the blue miseries, just a-setting around the place, till one day she cut herself with a kitchen knife and damn near bled to death. After that they put her in the nigger hospital near Saint Lou.

"I called on her a few times, but she had changed so much in there I could scarcely recognize her." Moses chewed his grass and looked down the hill. "And she didn't know me at all. Her spirit had done died with that chile. She grew to a old woman in six months' time in that place, and never knew me at all.

"I still don't know if I done the right thing, leaving her there. I think about that damn near every day. Fact, for a long time I hated myself for that. But I expect even the soul can heal.

"So I left off preaching and left the city life and come back here where I reckon I belong. I ain't never heard what become of her, but for me she done died long ago. I just hope they took good care of that suffering old woman that was left in her place."

The men fell silent once more, each with his own thoughts.

Chance broke the silence. "Like so much liverwurst," he said.

Black Moses gaped. "Say, *what?*"

Chance looked up. "I'm sorry," he said. "Just thinking about someone I knew once."

Black Moses shook his head. "Well ain't you something," he said.

Chance had watched in silence while Moses talked. He was struck by the complexity of the past that seemed to drive this man, though toward what kind of future he could not tell.

"So you left the city and the Lord and come back to punching cows."

Moses stared at him again for a moment. He seemed to be weighing fateful prospects.

"No," he said at last, "a man cain't hardly leave the Lord, much as he might try. I expect the Lord have watched over me about as good as a man could hope, though I got to wonder what was on his mind when he sent me you."

"Every blessing brings a new cross to bear," Chance said.

"Mmm, mm, mm," said Black Moses.

Moses stood and walked a little along the crest of the hill, getting a good look down along their trail. He walked with a stiff-legged hitch. Stars were beginning to appear in the evening sky.

"I don't suppose this here leg will ever be the same again," Moses said. "Even seem to feel shorter now. Work pretty good for everything it's been through, but it sho' do stiffen up on me now."

He returned to where Chance still sat. "We might as well set here till night come on," he said. "After that, anybody track us in the dark can have us." He looked down at Chance. "Seem to me we started this here story of my life talking about what we gon' do next."

Chance plucked a stalk of grass as Moses had done, but did not put it in his mouth. "So we did," he said. He looked away toward the mountains now just visible beyond the terrible veil of smoke and shifting light. "Next," he said. "I guess it would help to know more about what's north of here."

Moses sat back down where he had been. "We could go east to the trail and down into Laszlo's place the way other folks go. Only danger that way is other folks."

"Hm," Chance said. "But whatever is going on up ahead is tied to everything else. I want to know."

"Ain't you trying to get to Laszlo's, or what?"

"I'll get to Laszlo's, dammit, but I need to know what's going on in these hills. You don't seem much concerned."

"I told you I'd get you to Laszlo's," Moses said, "but I aim to keep my skin on too. We can probably get down to Laszlo's that way, but a lot depend on who we stumble over while we tryin'."

Chance broke into a wide grin. "Then let's not stumble," he said.

"Laszlo a strange one." Moses said. "I've always been fine just leaving him be, though I reckon there ain't no real harm in the man."

"Do you think he knows as much about the basin as folks say?"

"Oh, he know plenty. But he a strange one. A foreign man. Got a suspicious eye. I expect I'll let you do the talking."

Chance paused for a moment. "Swannie knows me," he said.

"He know you?"

"He said he knows who I am."

"Know you for what?"

Chance did not reply. He was so close to the answer he could touch it. He was so close to the answer he could almost take it in his hand.

"Whatever happens now," he said, "there's two things I have to know: who had Bagley killed, and who I am."

"You mean who you was."

"Was, is . . . It's all the same to me."

"But why you got to know who you was to know who you is? Don't seem to me to make no nevermind."

"How can I look to the future without the past? It's not just the dream of a great ranch, or whether I have a debt to collect; I need to know whether I have one to pay. I have to know what kind of man I am."

"But what difference it make now who you was then? That's gone. The future ain't nothing but a handful of maybes—maybe you ought to choose one that ain't tied to a dead past, and just get on with your life."

"But the future that brought me here is worthless without its past. I can't choose it if it isn't true—but if it is, I must."

"Why? It's up to you whether you choose it or not. What if you find that you really was robbed? What are you going to do about it now? And what if you find out that you was the evil son? Or that you just run out and left your daddy to die? Maybe you be better off just starting over. Lot of mens wish they could."

Chance examined his grass.

"Don't misunderstand," Moses said. "Every man got to have his hope. But the stronger your hopes, the tougher the choices you got to make. That's how a good man distinguish himself from the rest: by his choices. I expect you got some choosing to do."

Moses stood up and walked stiffly again along the crest of the hill. "Well," he said, "I sho' don't see no posse. Getting dark. Maybe we best get on back."

They got their horses and rode back down into their little dell.

"Yaas, a man got to have his dreams," Moses said almost

204

to himself. "But he owe it to himself and everybody else to weigh his dreams, and consider what they gon' cost."

Moses dismounted and picked up his bedroll from where he had left it earlier. "I expect we be wise to spread out again tonight," he said. "And Lord, am I gon' sleep."

Chance carried his own gear to the other end of the pond and up the hill to some trees. The air was redolent of grasses and dry earth. He laid out his bedding in a sandy spot where he could see the sky, then walked back to where Moses was taking off his boots.

"You ain't sleeping with your boots on," he said.

"Hell, no. I told you, if they can ketch me now they can have me." Moses lay back and pulled his blanket up to his chin. "Gon' be cold tonight," he said.

Chance traced a line in the sand with the toe of his boot. "Look," he said, "you don't seem to think I've chosen very well."

Moses didn't move, except to fold his hands behind his head. "I'm just adding up the costs," he said. "Seem to me they done ran pretty high already, and you still don't even know if you know what you want to know."

"But don't I owe it to myself to find out? And what about those who went before me? He was my father—don't I owe him that much?"

Moses rose a little and looked up at Chance. "Your father dead and gone, man. You gon' have to decide for yourself whose dreams you gon' follow, and who you gon' be. And whatever dreams you follow, they may want sacrifice and all. But your sacrifices gon' have to be your own. Don't no man have the right to sacrifice nobody else. For nothin.'"

Chance walked away a few steps, then looked up at the hills.

"Follow this maybe of yours," Moses said, "if that's what you got to do. Go ahead and search for your past and your future and whatever else you got to search for. But stop

205

now and then and consider whether you doing right."

"Doing right," Chance said.

"Don't take but two tests—Whether you keeping your commitments, and whether you easing pain or causing it." Moses lay back again with his hands behind his head. "And whether you letting folks get they sleep."

"That's three," Chance said.

Moses goggled. "All right," he said, "three! Now get your raggedy ass out of here before I start causing some pain myself."

XXIX

WHEN CHANCE AWOKE, THE SUN WAS ALREADY UP. He had slept hard. His body and his mind were both numb.

Moses had risen first and had been to the hill to check their trail. "No one coming," Moses said. "I expect we shook 'em yesterday morning. That's one worry off our minds. Could have turned bad, us sleeping half the day like this."

"Felt good," Chance said. "What's for grub?"

"Sun-warmed water rat, if you can ketch one. Otherwise I got the last of Swannie's corn. Just one can. We can knife fight for it if you game."

"Wouldn't be fair, you being an aging cripple and all. I'll just kill a snake or two."

Moses opened the can with his knife and ate half, then gave the rest to Chance. They lashed their gear back on the horses and started up the hill, traversing toward the east. Behind them to the south there was no sign of pursuit.

They were in high country now, with sweeping views of the badlands to the east. Chance's side hurt more than it had the day before; the long night on the ground had made it stiff. The other hurt, the one inside, was another matter.

Late in the morning they reached the top of that country. The hills to the north dropped away toward the plains of the Missouri. Below them lay the rift up which Chance had followed the trail of the stolen cattle, and the pass where he had first been fired upon.

They were well above the pass and half a mile away. The valley into which the cattle trail had disappeared lay ahead of them to the right. It was the canyon of the creek that flowed from the pond where they had spent the night.

Moses looked the country over, then dismounted and took his horse by the reins. "Let's poke around on foot a while," he said. "No use skylining ourselves before we know who else around." He led his horse to a stand of pines down the slope to the south and east of the crest. Chance followed.

They drew their carbines and took long drinks, then agreed to split up. Chance wanted to steal down to the pass. He knew from experience that a lookout or an ambush could set up there, and he wanted to see for himself. Moses planned to contour to the east for a better view of the valley and the pass.

Chance approached the pass down a shallow gully, then edged around a thicket of greasewood for a better look. That was when he saw the horse. Less than fifty yards below him to his right a saddled grulla grazed on an open slope. Its rider was not in sight. Keeping a rocky shelf to his left, he crept toward the open slope on his right for a better look.

As he reached the end of the rocks, the silence of the place shattered like a dropped jug. He saw the snake coiling in the rocks to his left and skipped away backward up the hill, raising enough commotion to bring a rustler brigade.

From the shelter of the greasewood he looked back to see what he had stirred up. The horse was nervous now because of the snake. Chance was nervous too. The rider was still nowhere to be seen.

Chance stole into the draw and made his way back to his own horse. Moses was waiting.

"You see him?" Moses said.

"Saw his horse," Chance said. "Couldn't find him." He didn't mention the snake.

"Just below you," Moses said. "*Damn*, man, I thought you was fixing to pick his pocket. He was watching the pass, just like you figured. Must have been asleep."

"That means there's others up here too. And cattle, probably."

"Ain't no cattle in the valley, and it's too steep to drive them down, so they got to be up somewheres across from the pass."

"That's what I figure," Chance said. "There's a creek that drops into the valley from beyond the hill just across the way. Must be a canyon back in there. Looked like cattle could be driven that way easy enough."

"That's where they at, then. Probably men, too. That's why they got this lookout posted so far back this way, watching their backtrail. But they ain't expecting no one to come slunkin' out of these hills—so that's just what we gon' do."

They rode down into the creek to the east. They forded the creek, then dismounted to water the horses.

To the north the creek dropped off into the valley of meadows and groves, but where they were it came down through a long defile between the hills. Green grass sprouted near the creek, and solitary pines grew along the hills. A band of low cliffs slashed the hillside about a hundred feet above them.

The water in the creek was clear and fast. The bottom of the creek was covered with pebbles and stones that seemed to dart and move in the stream. The men were as thirsty as the animals, and the water was cold and good.

They filled their canteens, then mounted and angled up to the right around the cliffs. At the top of a broad ridge they turned north again and continued to climb. They kept to the right of the ridge so they would not be seen from across the way. And they were careful not to kick up dust.

209

They stopped in a notch near the top of the hill.

"You think this rustling camp just over yonder?" Moses asked.

"That's the way she looked," Chance said. "About the only place she could be."

"Well, I expect I'll crawl over that way for a peek. If there's a canyon over there they using for cattle, it must have another outlet. What I want you to do is head over east with the horses and see what you can find. Two things we ought to know: do they have a way out over there—and do we?"

"Wouldn't we do better to wait for nightfall before we go poking around any more?"

"Oh, I expect so, but I'd like to see the lay of the place before it get too dark. Just make sho' nobody see *you*. And don't scare up no more snakes."

"Don't you want to leave your horse here?"

"No, just be a nuisance. I ruther be on foot a while."

"And what are you planning to do while I'm herding livestock all across the wilderness?"

"Just what I said. If I can, I'll get a look at the way of things over there so's we'll know what we getting into. Get as good a look as you can at that end of the situation. I'll ketch up with you there."

Chance didn't have a better plan, so he agreed.

Moses unsheathed his Winchester again and took a field glass from a saddlebag, then started for the top of the hill. Chance led Moses' big bay gelding out of the notch on a downward contour toward the east. He didn't like splitting up like that, but he could see the point.

The ridgeline of the hill above him dropped as he worked his way east, and he dropped with it, staying below the crest. East of him and south the hills fell away to the badlands beyond.

The ridge bottomed out in a meadow ringed by trees. Chance left the horses up the hill a way and moved down into the meadow on foot. The far side of the meadow was bounded by a rocky knoll; to the southeast the knoll and meadow dropped away into a wide ravine. There was no sign of traffic through the meadow.

Chance skirted the meadow, staying to the trees, and rounded the foot of the ridge. Before him opened the mouth of a canyon, just as he had expected. The canyon ran back to the west, then broke to the left. Chance could see what looked like less than half its length. What he could see looked like a good place for cattle.

And cattle there were.

Pole fences had been strung across the mouth of the canyon. One ran about seventy-five feet from the foot of the ridge to the flank of the rocky knoll. Across the way another ran from the knoll to the opposite hill. Chance could see about a hundred head of cattle, all young.

He slipped back to his meadow and circled it toward the south. The gully that led out of the hills looked like a usable escape. A rider could drop south down the ravine and east to the main trail, and probably miss the cattle trail altogether.

He circled behind the rocky knoll until he came to the other pole fence, and the other mouth of the canyon.

It was the cattle trail, all right. A large opening between the knoll and the opposite hill led to open slopes along the foot of the range, just as he had guessed, and from there to other ranges.

From that point Chance could see farther back along the canyon. It was about a thousand yards long and a hundred-fifty yards wide. A stand of aspen on the north side, at about the dogleg, indicated a spring, the source of the stream he had seen. Whoever was using the place had twenty or thirty acres of good bottom with grass and water.

Not a soul was in sight. Chance looked up along the southern flank of the canyon for some sign of Moses. The

211

wall was not steep, but like the opposite side was mostly open—an unlikely place for a sneak approach. There was no sign of Black Moses.

Chance turned and made his way back to the horses. Moses was not there. He took a drink from his canteen and gave some water to the horses, then climbed the hill a little way and found a place beside a boulder where he could keep an eye on them.

He sat down. He was hungry. He hadn't eaten since breakfast, and that hadn't been much. He thought of the bacon Moses had with his gear, but decided he still wasn't quite that hungry.

Even more than food he wanted coffee, and just as much he wanted a smoke. He had used up all his tobacco, and Moses did not smoke. He did not want a drink. He thought about waking up drunk two or three nights before, and about the things that had been unfolding even then, and about Maggie finding him like that when she came to warn him of those things.

Never again, he thought. He could not live without coffee or smoke, but he would never drink again.

A cold foreboding began to settle over the place. The sun had gone behind the hill, and the country to the east was throwing tall shadows upon itself. The shadows grew like spirits as Chance watched.

And still Moses did not appear.

Men were probably camped in the canyon. The sentry at the pass was theirs; he would most likely come back to camp at dusk. A night watch would be posted at the mouth of the canyon and probably another by the fences.

There was not much he and Moses could do alone against a camp of armed cowthieves. They could not even get the information they had back to town.

Everything pointed to Laszlo. He had to get down to Laszlo's.

212

A cool breeze drifted off the hill. Dusk descended like a spell. But Moses did not come.

Chance looked around to be sure he was alone, then stood up and stretched his legs. *Son of a bitch should be here by now*, he thought. *He should have been here hours ago.* Chance picked up a stone the size of his fist and threw it at the trunk of a pine down the hill. *Goddamn colored*, he thought. *I never asked him to follow me up here in the first place.*

He thought of going for help. Down to Laszlo's. He didn't like it there on that hillside. He didn't want to travel in the dark; there was bad country below him, country he didn't know. Yet the notion clattered through his brain that he could make it down to Laszlo's if he left right away.

He moved the horses to a spot with a little more graze, then as darkness gathered, started up the hill on foot.

From the top of the ridge he could see the whole eastern end of the canyon, probably two hundred feet below him. He could hear the cattle lowing. There were still no signs of men.

About four hundred yards to his left the hill extended into the canyon, forming the dogleg he had seen from below. He could not see the canyon beyond the bend.

He crawled back from the crest of the ridge and started for the top of the hill, just above the bend. He moved carefully; he was not far from the last place he had seen Moses.

Just below the summit he explored an area of scattered rocks for signs of Moses. No one was there. Nothing.

And no one on the top of the hill.

He crept over the top and looked down. The hill fell away steeply at first, then more gently as it dropped into the canyon.

He could see the whole canyon now. Below him, just left of the dogleg, was a fire.

He watched the camp for several minutes. A handful of

men stood or sat around the fire. From that distance they were hard to count, but Chance believed there were five or six. There seemed to be others lying on the ground, asleep already, or passed out. The voices of the men rose on the night air. Chance could not quite make out what they said. From time to time there was laughter.

One of the men was building a second fire near the edge of the camp, building it for some reason under a tree. When he had the fire going, two of the men hoisted something by a rope from a branch of the tree so that it hung just over the fire. The thing looked like a side of veal, but something told Chance it was not.

He looked around. There was still no sign of anyone else on the hill. As he looked back down at the camp, one of the men by the fire called out.

"Hey, Broken-face," the man called out. His voice echoed in the canyon but carried like a silver note on the quiet air. Chance stared through the night. They knew he was there. They even knew who he was.

"Broken-face!" the man called again. "Listen. We have your friend Sixapikwan." Laughter rose from the other men. "We have the black white-man. But we are finished with him now. Come and get him."

The men were Indians. Cutthroat bandits, Chance thought, renegades most likely from one of the reservations.

He decided to go. There was nothing he could do for Moses now. He had to get out of there before they came looking for him. He thought of the horses; without them he would be as dead as Moses.

He crawled back from the brow of the hill and looked around, then crept down to where he had traversed with the horses earlier and followed their tracks to where he had left them. They were still there.

He knew the men could be waiting for him below, at the meadow—but to stay where he was to wait for them to

214

come to him, and in the light of morning the hunt would be easy.

He thought with regret of Black Moses. He hadn't even wanted him to come. And he wondered whether Laszlo too might have fallen victim to these men. It was time to find out.

He led the horses down the ridge toward the meadow that marked the route of his escape. He stayed between them, the appaloosa to his right.

He kept to the fringe of the meadow with the horses. At the head of the ravine he climbed into the saddle, then glanced back toward the mouth of the canyon.

As he started down the draw, he glanced back once more. "Damn it all to hell," he said.

He pulled up and dismounted, then led the horses back through the meadow and up the hill a way and tethered them in the trees below the place they had been before. Then he started up the hill.

At the top of the hill he looked down again into the camp. He could no longer see the men in the camp, and the fires had burned down. He did not believe the men had gone to bed. They might have cleared out to lure him into the trap. Or they might by then have drunk themselves senseless. The men who had passed out earlier still slept near the fire.

Moses was dead, Chance was certain, but dead or alive, he deserved better than to be left with those men. Even so, Chance had someplace else he needed to be, and time was against him now.

The whole thing made his head spin. He knew he had some choosing to do.

Near the bottom of the hill he picked his way into some trees a few yards from the camp. There was no sign of life anywhere, not even horses. He edged closer to the camp. The dangling form of the body in the tree was gruesome in the dark.

He circled the camp looking for its inhabitants. They were gone. He wondered if they were looking for him.

The two senseless bodies still lay in the dust near the campfire. Chance shook his head—how long it seemed. He prodded one of them with his boot. The man groaned and rolled over toward Chance.

Chance stood bolt upright. The man was not an Indian. And he was not a stranger. The man was his own foreman, Fil Hazzard.

Fil was not sleeping. And Fil was not drunk. Terrible things had been done to him, unspeakable things. He lay in the dust and moaned as his life ebbed away.

The other man was already dead. Chance believed he knew him too, the gunslinger Vasner Stanche. Stanche had been shot in the back.

Chance turned to the hanging-tree. Black Moses dangled by his feet above the burned-out fire.

Chance cut him down and laid him on the ground. Moses was barely recognizable from the fire. Chance hoped he had died before he was hanged.

He looked around again, still expecting some surprise, but there was none. The desperados were gone. They had left this grisly spectacle just for him; they had given him the horror of finding it for himself.

He walked to the creek and got some water in his hat, then sprinkled a little in Fil Hazzard's face.

"Fil," he said. "Fil."

Fil shook his head. "Don't," he said.

"Fil it's me, Chance. What happened?"

"Chance?" he said. "Oh, Jesus. Chance? I told him not to, Chance."

"You told who, Fil?"

Fil seemed to want to answer, but couldn't seem to find his tongue. He lay in the dirt and moved his lips and said nothing.

216

"Who did you tell, Fil?"

Fil lay on his back in the dust. "Bert," he whispered.

"Bert? What did you tell him?"

Fil Hazzard moved his lips. He seemed to be whispering something to the night, but Chance could not make out what he said.

"What did you tell him, Fil?"

Fil lay in the dirt. "Don't," he said, struggling for breath.

"Don't what, Fil?"

Fil tried weakly, almost stupidly, to move his arm.

"What are you trying to say, Fil? You mean this?" Chance looked around. "All this?"

Fil struggled for breath. "This," he said.

"You mean this operation was Bert's? All this? And you were in on it?"

"I told him not to." Fil struggled. "Bad," he said, and struggled for breath.

"And Stanche? He was in this with you and Bert?"

"Stanche," Fil said.

"Fil, listen. Did Stanche kill Bagley? Did Stanche murder that stranger for Bert?"

"Stanche," he whispered. "For Bert." He groaned pitifully.

"Jesus Christ, Fil. And you were in on it?"

"Please," Fil groaned. "Please."

Chance waited. Fil Hazzard only groaned. "Please," he groaned.

"Please what?" Chance said.

"Please," Fil said again.

"What, Fil?"

"Please," was all he said. He stared up from the ground. "Please." He licked his lips, then took a breath as if to speak again, then groaned. "Please," he said.

And finally Chance understood.

He thought of letting Fil Hazzard die slowly. He couldn't believe what the man had done.

217

"Okay," Chance said. "But I have to know. Was this rustling Bert's? Did these men work for him? Did Stanche?"

"Bert's," Fil said. "All Bert's. Please."

Chance rolled Fil Hazzard back on his face and shot him through the head.

He left Hazzard and Stanche where they lay. Soon they would be dust. Perhaps their souls would wander the hills in search of peace. He hoped they never found it.

He began to worry that the shot would bring more trouble. He wasn't sure he really cared, but he thought he should get going.

He hoisted the body of Black Moses over his shoulder and started down the canyon toward the horses.

XXX

THE TROUBLES OF OUR PROUD AND ANGRY DUST
are from eternity, the poet Housman said. But they find us
where we are—and they find us wherever we go.

North of the badlands the hill country fell away toward
the plains of the Missouri. The land was dry, but yielded
sheep grass and occasional water. And sheep.

Chance spotted Laszlo's shack half a mile below him. It
sat on a bench where the hills ran out onto the plains.
Chance watched the shack for signs of life as he rode down
out of the hills. He didn't see any.

The cabin was as dry and rude as the land around it,
and very old, a sun-bleached hovel with a sod roof.

Chance pulled up and watched the shack before he approached. He could see no horse or mule, no dog, no other
sign of life. He hailed the cabin, but no one came forth.

He rode down and tethered the horse to a hitchrack. He
knocked at the door, then went in. The place was lived in,
but Laszlo was not home.

He went back out and crossed to Laszlo's well. He drew
water and tended the horses, then took the body of Moses
from the bay. He returned with Moses to the shack and laid

219

him on Laszlo's bunk. He told himself the sheepherder would not mind.

Moses was bent double from being carried over the horse. Chance straightened him out as well as he could to make him lie on the bunk.

He found a pick and shovel among Laszlo's gear and set to digging a grave for Moses. He was tired and hungry; he had not eaten or slept in over a day. But he had it in his mind that he would not rest until Moses had been laid to rest.

He dug the hole both wide and deep in the heat of the midday sun, and when he had it deep enough he took up the body of Black Moses and laid it in the grave.

He climbed out of the hole, then stood at the edge and looked down. He wanted to curse this man for what he had done. But he could not.

"O Palinarus," he said, remembering some lines of Virgil, "Too well didst thou trust a calm of heaven and sea." He bent over and picked up a handful of dust, then scattered it into the grave. "But thou shalt not lie a naked corpse on some unknown shore." He filled in the grave, then erected a wooden cross, the proper thing, he thought, for a minister of the Word.

He finished caring for the horses, then returned to the cabin to wait for Laszlo. In spite of the heat he started a fire. He cut Moses' bacon slab in half and sliced one of the halves for frying. He realized that this would probably be the last thing he ever got from Swanson Johnson.

He boiled a little of Laszlo's coffee and helped himself to a little of Laszlo's tobacco, then took a seat on a bench outside to watch for Laszlo's return.

He dozed while he waited, and woke in shadow with the cool of evening coming on. He was still alone.

He looked around the place. Laszlo had just been there, probably that morning. There was no sign the cutthroats had been there. Their trail, he thought, ran west of a long

220

hill some four or five miles distant, and brought them nowhere near this place. He remembered the distance Indians were said to have given Laszlo and his ways.

He watched for Laszlo, and waited, but no one came.

When darkness fell he lay down on Laszlo's bunk. He thought of its most recent occupant, but he didn't care; he was all but dead himself from fatigue and regret.

He waited the following day with the same result. He did some work on the place, but mostly he thought.

His quest of the destiny he had sought was a blue ruin. Even if Laszlo showed up and told him everything he had ever wanted to know, where would that leave him now? Nothing had worked out. There was no way on earth to go back now. The costs had been too high after all.

So he waited for Laszlo. Paradise would stay lost, but at least maybe Laszlo would give him the truth—and maybe the truth, at last, would set him free.

That evening he shot a rabbit and fried it up in the bacon grease he had saved. And he waited for Laszlo. He wondered how long he would have to wait.

We forge our own destinies; or so the argument goes. But that argument is not quite true either: in forging our own destinies we also shape the destinies of those around us even as they, in forging theirs, shape ours. A paradox; an absurdity. Yet if there is any truth in it, it is both our ruin and our salvation.

Shortly after noon Chance spotted a rider coming down from those sheep-wrangler hills. He took up his carbine and stood in the doorway to wait.

The man rode a tall horse with an awkward gait. He sat a little awkwardly in the saddle as well, almost sideways, thinking perhaps of turning back.

221

As Chance watched the man approach, he noticed a dry buzzing in the air, a faint and dusty jingling, as if ten thousand parched cicadas sang somewhere in the brush just out of hearing.

The man reined up a little beyond rifle range and looked the situation over. Then he rode in.

The man did not look like any kind of European; he was an Indian of some sort, probably part white. He wore a sombrero so flat and dusty it could have been the lair of the east wind. Almost everything else, his shirt and his pants and his boots, were shabby and old, and in spite of the heat he wore an ancient serape over his shoulder.

Chance was uncertain of the man's age. He had a roundish face unlike any of the plains people, Chance thought, and was missing two or three front teeth.

"I don't think I know you," the man said.

"I'm waiting for Laszlo," Chance said.

"That's what I figured."

"I don't guess you're him," Chance said. "You're too young."

"Plus being a Indian," the man said, and grinned. His voice was soft, almost hollow, and he spoke with a lilt that made his sentences sound like questions. He formed his words with care around his missing teeth; his speech was the verbal equivalent of squinting.

"Climb down," Chance said, "set a spell."

"I don't think so," the man said, looking around. "I see you buried somebody."

"Yes. A friend of mine."

"Who was it?"

"A man named Black Moses."

"I knew him. He was okay. What got him?"

Chance thought for a moment. "Destiny," he said.

The man showed a half-toothless grin.

"I've been waiting here a couple days," Chance said. "You know Laszlo? Know where he is?"

"I still don't know you," the man said.

Chance hesitated to tell him, but decided it didn't matter.

"Name's Chance," he said. "Yours?"

"Moses," the man said. "People call me Red Moses."

"Moses!" Chance said. He pushed his hat back to scratch his head.

"I used to have another name," Red Moses said, "but nobody calls me by that one any more."

"And what was that?"

"I don't think you could pronounce it."

"Try me."

Red Moses grinned his toothless grin and said something Chance could not understand, much less pronounce. For a moment Chance believed he saw the sun, the moon, and the east wind in that grin.

"Maybe I've seen you before," Red Moses said.

"Where? Around here?"

"I can't remember. Maybe so."

"Do you live in these parts?"

"All around here." He waved his arm in the general direction of the horizon.

"Have you lived here long?"

"All my life."

Chance's heart was too tired to pound much any more, but he felt it pick up a beat just the same. "Maybe we met around here some years back," he said. "Maybe over in the basin."

"Could be. I can't remember, but your face looks familiar."

"Tell me this. Did you know Will Johnson or Millard Quackenbush in the old days?"

"Sure. Everybody did."

"Tell me about them."

"They were crazy. They thought they could be king. They

223

both wanted to be king of all this place around here, but they couldn't both be king, so—" He shrugged.

"So what?"

"They destroyed each other."

"I guess so. Did the Johnsons murder Quackenbush?"

"No."

"Well, who did?"

Moses' grin spread like rangefire across the wilderness of his face.

"Destiny," he said.

"Well you're a shit load of help," Chance said, "but at least tell me this, okay? If you can. Will Johnson had a son, and maybe the son will be king one day. Did Quackenbush have a son?"

"Quackenbush? Yes, I remember somebody."

"Somebody? A son?"

Red Moses seemed to study Chance's face again for a moment. "It wasn't no daughter," he said.

"I've even heard that he had two sons. A good one and a bad. Could that be true?"

"Could be, I suppose. Anything is possible around here."

"What became of them? Where are they now? Do you know?"

"The one I heard of was sent somewheres for school and nobody ever seen him again. I think I heard one time that he died—but maybe that was the other one, you know?"

"How about Laszlo? Would he know any more than that?"

"Might."

"Maybe I'll ask him myself. Do you know when he'll be back?"

"No."

"Do you know where he is?"

"I don't think he'll be back today."

"Maybe tomorrow?"

"I don't think so."

224

"Well, what . . . ? When did he leave here, do you know that?"

"A couple days ago."

"But you don't know when he'll be back?"

"He may not come back at all."

"Not come back! You mean he's left? He's dead? He's . . . what?"

"I think so."

Chance took off his hat and threw it into the dust and gawked at this man in disbelief. "You mean that's all you're going to tell me?" he shouted.

Red Moses shrugged. "I can't tell you what I don't know," he said. Then he grinned once more. His grin seemed to augur an infinite progression of mysteries. Chance became aware once more of the strange chirring that hung in the air like insect electricity.

A notion sprang up in Chance's thoughts.

"You're Laszlo's boy, aren't you? Laszlo's son."

Red Moses looked off to the north as if he hoped to spot something on the horizon, then turned back and looked down at Chance. "I don't talk much about myself," he said. "It's bad luck."

He looked back toward the horizon, then turned his idiotic grin on Chance once more. "Well," he said. "Maybe I'll see you." He turned away again, then chucked his horse up and rode off with that peculiar gait toward the big sky distance in the north.

The world stands on absurdities. Maybe in the end the best we can do is embrace the absurd and make it ours.

Shortly before dusk Chance spotted a rider coming down from those sheep-wrangler hills. He took up his carbine and stood in the doorway to wait.

The man rode a tall horse with an awkward gait. He sat

225

a little awkwardly in the saddle as well, almost sideways, thinking perhaps of turning back.

As Chance watched the man approach, he noticed a dry buzzing in the air, a faint and dusty jingling, as if ten thousand parched cicadas sang somewhere in the brush just out of hearing.

The man reined up a little beyond rifle range and looked the situation over. Then he rode in.

In the gathering dark Chance could not make out the man's face. He was tall and old and wore a sombrero so flat and dusty it could have been the lair of the east wind. Almost everything else, his shirt and his pants and his boots, were shabby and worn, and in spite of the heat he wore an ancient serape over his shoulder.

The man sat astride the tall horse. "I don't know you any more," he said. Insect electricity jingled in the air.

"You never did," Chance said. "But I know who I am."

"Know who you are," his father snorted. "And when did that ever matter before?"

"It matters now."

"I'm glad to hear that. What is your plan?"

"I guess that depends on whether I'm the good son or the bad one."

The old man snorted again. "Good son," he said with bitterness and looked out toward the dark horizon. "Good, bad, it's all the same. Indifferent, I'd say." He looked down at Chance. "There's only one of you. Never was more than one, and you're it. But time has a way of catching up, don't it? So I'll ask you again: What's your plan?"

"I don't think that's the real question, is it? Seems to me the real question is, What's *your* plan?"

"Your sarcasm has never served you well. You have an unfulfilled obligation. Your destiny has waited on you long enough. But you're planning to run away again, aren't you?"

"I've spent my life running from you. I'm not running any more. You don't give a damn about my destiny—it's yours you're worried about."

"Blood is destiny. My destiny is yours, and I aim to know what you plan to do about it. What about our place?"

"There is no place any more. It's gone."

"You're a chicken-livered whore-chaser, and you plan to run away again."

"No. I know better than that now. I know who I am. And I know who you are. I won't tell my own father to go to hell—but I don't think I have to. *Adios*, old man. I won't look for you again."

Chance looked down at his feet. He stood in a bed of dust. When he looked up his father was gone.

Chance set out that night and rode through the morning. After a long *siesta* he waited for dark, then rode into town to the back of Maggie's store. His quest of the destiny he had sought was gone like a puff of blue smoke, but still he had two things to do in that country. This was one of the things.

He knocked on the door of Maggie's kitchen. The look on her face was worth the risk he had taken to come. She pulled him quickly into the kitchen and shut the door.

"What are you doing here?" she said. She seemed to have been in bed; she was wearing a dressing gown and a pair of shapeless slippers. She was rather plain just then, Chance thought—yet very pretty.

"I just came for a cup of coffee," he said. "I ain't had any coffee in days."

In spite of the fear on her face, she laughed. "Chance, you shouldn't be here," she said. "They're still looking for you."

"I reckon," he said.

"They still say you killed that man Bagley, and now they're saying you burned the Big Grassy as well."

227

"I didn't burn it, but I was there. I suppose some would say it happened because of me."

He told her everything that had happened since the night she had come to his room. He told her how Bagley had come for him because Bagley had loved Elizabeth better than he had, and all the rest, to the deaths of Moses and Hazzard and Stanche and about Bert and finally about Laszlo and Red Moses. Maggie made coffee for him as he talked.

"What I still don't understand," he said, "is why you came to my room that night. It just don't make sense. What if I really had killed a man?"

Maggie put her hand on Chance's arm and looked into his face with her funny, pretty face. "I didn't think you were the killing type," she said quietly, "and I didn't like what I was hearing on the street. And after seeing you in your room I knew. You were in no condition, my friend—you couldn't have killed anyone that night."

Chance looked quickly down. "I wish you hadn't seen me like that," he said. "I hadn't touched a drop in two years. I picked a hell of a time to liquor up."

She said nothing, but watched him with her limpid pale eyes.

"Well," he said.

"Yes. What will you do now?"

"I reckon it's time to leave Montana. But there is one thing I'd like you to do. I want you to go to the sheriff tomorrow and tell him what I've told you about the rustling and how to find that canyon and about Fil and Stanche and Bert, and about Moses."

"How should I tell him I found all this out?"

"Just tell him the truth. Tell him I came here to see you one last time and asked you to pass this on."

"Chance, I can't imagine that he'll believe it."

"Neither can I, but it's the truth and it's got to be told, and I'm sure not the one to do the telling. I expect all this

228

could open the door to certain investigations that might prove adverse to the fortunes of the Rocking Tree Ranch."

"But if I tell him, he'll send someone to track you down."

"Maybe, but by morning I'll be gone. Don't go to him till then, but go in the morning. Will you do that?"

She looked at him. "Yes," she said.

"I'm counting on you," he said. Then he looked into his cup and swirled it a little in the way of someone he had once cared about. "One other thing," he said. "You're my only friend now. That means everything to me."

She looked into his eyes and let her gaze shift from one to the other, back and forth, then put her hands on his. There was something in her face he had not seen this side of death. It was something he knew he liked.

"Me too," she said.

"I'll write to you," he said.

"But they'll find you."

"Oh, maybe. I'm going to Canada. I'll get some business envelopes made up, mercantile supply or some such. And a new name. If you start getting familiar letters from an unfamiliar source, you'll know."

She squeezed his hands and smiled. "Yes," she said. "I'll watch for them."

"Maggie, if there's ever anything you need—I can't tell you how important this is to me. I will always be your friend."

He rose and drew her to her feet, then put his arms around her and held her for a long minute. He kissed her quickly on the lips, then stepped away.

"I have to go now," he said.

"I'll go to Jack in the morning. God speed."

He picked up his hat and stepped to the door, then turned back. "Maggie, there's one more thing. I have to tell you this. There is one more thing I have to do before I go. I . . . I'm afraid you may not think it's too good a thing."

"Chance . . ."

"I won't hurt nobody," he said. "I promise you. But it's something I have to do."

"Oh, Chance," she said as the look of fear rose back into her face.

He held her by the arms and kissed her once more, a little longer and more tenderly than before, then let her go and stepped back. "Just tell Jack in the morning," he said, and slipped out Maggie's door.

Chance rode wide of the Rocking Tree in the dark, then came around from the north. He left the appaloosa out of sight of the ranch by a stand of trees that ran north along the foot of the mountains.

Two dogs came out to investigate, but he knew them both. They did not bark.

He went to the shed where he knew the lamp oil was kept. He found a jug of the stuff and carried it to where the house rose ominously in the dark.

As quietly as he could, he slopped the kerosene onto the house, on the great porches, front and back, on the wood-pile Bert kept on the back porch, on some lumber beside the house, on every place he could quietly reach that seemed like fuel.

When he had emptied the jug he looked up at the house, waiting like a sinister thought in the night, then lit the oil, first at the woodpile, then at the lumber by the side of the house, then at the front porch. When he saw that it was catching fire, he withdrew to the shelter of the trees.

He waited until he saw that the house itself was starting to burn, then fired his Colt into the air.

"Fire!" he shouted. Then he watched.

The flames rose up the sides of the house and engulfed the massive porches and spread to the roof, fed, it seemed, by the pure oxygen of retribution. In the light of the flames the silhouettes of men appeared, running this way and that, shouting and organizing a platoon.

Bert appeared, comical in his nightshirt, barking orders while shadow men scurried at his command. Chance raised his rifle and drew a bead on Bert. He had it in his heart to kill Bert Kaffo then and there.

But he had promised.

He lowered the carbine and watched.

Soon the great house of the Rocking Tree was overwhelmed by fire as flames embraced the dark Montana sky.

Chance was unable to leave. He watched in fascination the tremendous thing he had just done, the end, he thought, of a corrupt and powerful dream—powerful because it had been raised up out of the earth and was, after all, a dream of the human heart; yet corrupt, not because it had pretended to dominion over the land, but because it had placed itself above the other dreams and hopes and aspirations of the soul.

Yet it was not the end, either. He knew these places would be built again and men would continue their struggle for the power that fueled the building of the West.

But for Chance it was the end. Whatever the Sally Basin may once have been to him, or he to it, he knew the dream had been corrupt. He knew the dream had been a fool's paradise.

That dream was his no more. The raging blaze before him was an act of vengeance; yet not of vengeance only. It was a purging; yet it was an expiation as well, a reconciliation. He understood at last that the future really does decide the past.

He moved back through the trees to his horse. He mounted up, then started north.

An hour later he left the Sally Basin and rode out onto the plains. The fire still burned behind him, glowing orange now against the blackness of the mountains. But this time he knew the cause.

Jim Knisely was born and raised in Seattle, Washington. He studied writing at the University of Washington with Theodore Roethke and David Wagoner, and more recently with Jack Cady and at Richard Hugo House in Seattle. He holds degrees from Whitworth College and Princeton Theological Seminary. His publications include poetry, fiction and satire in *Summit, Point No Point,* and *Exquisite Corpse* magazines. He has worked as a backcountry fire fighter and a New York City youth worker, and is now a retired parole officer living in Seattle.